THE CLIFF HOUSE

part one

MURDERS UNDER THE SUN
SEASON ONE; INTRO

MOLLY: Welcome to *Murders Under the Sun*, a podcast that explores a series of unusual crimes that have occurred in sunny Southern California.

I'm Molly Shure, your host. For the past five years I've worked as a journalist at a local news outlet. Stories of murder and mayhem come across my desk weekly, if not daily. However, one day last March, I noticed something startling.

There seemed to be a connection between several crimes that transpired over a five year period—seven crimes to be precise. What connected them? Location for one. They all took place within a twenty-mile radius of each other, but that alone wasn't significant.

The thing that pinged in my brain was that many of the people at the center of these crimes knew each other. Not the criminals, which would be an obvious thread, but the victims. I know, I know, six degrees of separation. Didn't I already say the crimes took place in a twenty-mile radius? But we're not talking six degrees here. It's more like one degree.

You'll see if you stick with me for all seven seasons of the show, the crimes circle back around. The people you meet in the first season play a role in Season Seven's story.

Am I imagining things? Is the connection real? Is there one mastermind behind the crimes? Or are they linked by some kind of social, psychological or even spiritual force? I'm afraid that's something you'll have to decide for yourself.

Each season, I'll do a deep dive into just one

of these stories. You'll hear from the people who were victimized, and listen to transcripts of journal entries, memoirs, and letters from others who were involved—sometimes the criminals themselves—and behind-the-scenes information you can't get anywhere else.

So, get out your sunglasses. We're pulling back the curtains and letting the light shine on some of Orange County's darkest mysteries.

part two

MURDERS UNDER THE SUN
SEASON ONE; EPISODE ONE

MOLLY: Welcome to Season One of Murders Under the Sun. I'm Molly Shure, your host.

I've titled this season *The Cliff House*, because we'll be talking about the infamous Real Estate Killer. You may remember in 2017, a real estate agent named Sondra Olsen was killed in a vacant beach front property in Laguna Beach, California.

What transpired after her body was discovered threw the Orange County housing industry into a panic, and for good reason. It soon became apparent someone was targeting agents and brokers.

Gwen Bishop, an agent with Humboldt Realty, was at the center of these crimes. She graciously agreed to discuss her experience with me, but declined to be interviewed on air. Instead, I'll be relating what she told me in as personal a way as possible.

I've also located a never-before-released memoir from the actual Real Estate Killer. The literary agent who's working on selling his story to a publisher contacted me. I'm sure she wants the publicity and happily for us, REK is a total narcissist. He's delighted to have his story read to an audience.

Honestly, part of me hates giving him the airtime. But in light of the mission of this podcast series, I decided to hold my nose and read it to you. It adds a missing element, and may help us understand why he did what he did.

I won't be reading his entire manuscript, however. Only the sections I feel are needed to round out the victim's stories. REK's entries will be interspersed as they fit into the chronology of events. I think you'll find them as chilling as I do.

Let's begin this episode with one of the most terrifying of those entries.

Sometimes it's best to leave a door closed. When I crossed the threshold of my father's house on Cliff Drive, it changed me. Some would say not for the better.

I could argue my behavior was justified. We all have the right to protect our property from thieves and swindlers. But, really, it came down to simple lust. I was captivated by possibilities, and I wanted everything. I should have known by the screech of rusty hinges that door was better left shut.

I'd made an appointment to see the house as soon as it came on the market, about six months after my father's death. Sondra Olsen, local real estate agent, met me on the curb out front. She opened the gate I'd only passed through once before in my life. The old fig tree I remembered from that time was bigger now and mantled the court-yard like a vulture, obliterating the light and warmth from the late afternoon sun.

We traversed the walkway and came to the front door that had always been locked tight against me. She threw it open and ushered me in. The curved staircase that led to the part of the house reserved for the family—in other words, not me—rose before me without a barrier.

My initial feeling about Sondra was one of warmth. She and I were sharing in a momentous occasion. She dropped the drawbridge across the moat and invited me into the castle, so to speak. But as we toured the house, my opinion changed. Yes, she was pleasant, subservient even, but I began to see beneath the surface.

"It's a fixer, but it has so much charm, don't you think?" she asked with a dimpled smile.

"Yes, to both."

"Come look at the ocean view."

I paused before I stepped into the living room I'd only seen in bits and pieces through doors and windows. I don't know what I thought I'd find inside—the meaning of life, some kind of Holy Grail maybe.

"What do you think?" Sondra asked. I couldn't speak. It was a disappointment. A huge disappointment.

It was much smaller than I'd imagined. The lack of furniture revealed nicked and scarred wood flooring. Blank, dirty white walls framed the space. I didn't notice the cool breeze kissing my cheek until Sondra said, "Look at this view."

I walked through French doors onto a concrete patio and looked down on the beach where I'd so often stood. How many nights had I made my way across the sand or the water, depending on the tides, to bathe in the light emanating from these very doors? How many times had I sat on the rocks that looked so small from this vantage point, straining to catch a glimpse of the family within? His family. My family.

"Leaves you speechless, doesn't it?" Sondra said.

I turned to answer her and inhaled sharply. She was caught in a beam from the setting sun, just like another girl on another day. Her hair glowed like gold around her head and on the shoulders of her sky-blue dress. The vision only lasted for a moment. She turned and entered the house, and it was gone. But I recognized it as a premonition of sorts.

"The master bedroom has a terrific view, as well. Is there a partner? They'll love it if there is. Very romantic." She led me toward the foyer. Before heading up, I noticed a short, dark hallway to the left of the staircase.

"What's down there?" I pointed.

"Believe it or not, that's the basement. Most California homes don't have them, but this house stands on top of a series of small caves that tunnel into the cliff. The man who built this place in the forties was a shipping magnate and a collector of art, furniture, all kinds of things. When he found out about the caves, he commissioned an architect to create a warren of storage rooms."

"Is there anything in the rooms?" I asked.

"Probably, but don't worry. They'll be cleaned out before new owners move in."

"Can I see them?"

"The door is locked. I don't have a key." A cloud passed over Sondra's face as she said those words. She lied. It was my second clue. There must be a treasure within these disappointing walls after all.

"Let's go up, shall we?" She tilted her head and glanced at me from the corners of her eyes coquettishly, but it had no effect. She might as well have spit in my face. Unlike most men, I'm immune to the wiles of women.

I fingered the box cutter in my jacket pocket, then moved so quickly I surprised myself. I pulled her close and showed her the blade.

"Down," I said.

"In the kitchen. The...the...cellar keys are in the kitchen," she said. We shuffled into that room like geriatric ballroom dancers.

"The pantry." She gestured with her chin toward a door. A round key chain with several keys hung on a hook inside. We stumbled back to the foyer.

It took me three tries to find the correct key. Sondra was struggling the entire time. I had to get a little rough, but finally we descended the steep cellar steps together. Dim yellow lights revealed a long hallway with doors opening off it every ten feet or so. I twisted the knob of the first door on my right and nudged it open with my foot. A moldy funk wafted out.

A single bulb hanging in the center of the room exposed stone walls, slick with moisture and the shadowy outlines of furniture. Old tables, chairs, desks, and bureaus were stacked and jammed into every corner. Nothing looked particularly valuable. Just old oak.

We moved to the next door. I opened it and saw a mountain of cardboard boxes moldering on a damp floor. I stood Sondra in front of me, close enough to reach her if she moved, and opened one with my box cutter. I pushed aside the dusty cardboard and saw something that looked like peeling skin. I hesitated, then reached in and lifted the object. It was a woman's purse; or rather it had once been a purse. I dropped it in disgust.

"I told you. There is nothing here but trash," Sondra said.

I jerked her forward. The possibility she told the truth angered me more than her attempts to get me to leave off my search. I threw open door after door. The farther we went through the basement, the more enraged I became. My dream, the thing I'd longed for all these years, was nothing but a graveyard of old, decaying junk.

Sondra struggled against me. "Let me go. I won't tell anyone about this. I promise. Let's just go—"

"Shut up." I tightened my grip across her chest and nicked the smooth skin of her throat with the box cutter. She tensed, but stilled.

We came to the dead end of the hallway. I could hear the faint sound of waves throwing themselves against the cliff walls like they were seeking entrance. I kicked open the last door. The heavy wood bounced off the wall behind it. I dragged Sondra into the room, thinking I'd kill her here. Here at the dead end of my hopes. It would be my first time to kill a stranger, but I couldn't very well leave her alive after holding a box cutter to her throat.

I pushed the blade of my knife higher in its case. She began to fight in earnest now, scratching and biting. I threw her to the floor and fell on top of her. Her head slammed against the stone. She went limp.

As I sat panting, straddling her body, I saw it. Something glinted in the spill of light from the hallway. I stood to investigate. Joy dawned with realization. What was hidden here was better than I had ever imagined. It was an inheritance meant only for me. Maybe my father did think of me after all.

MOLLY: I told you his words were terrifying. It's not often we hear about a murder from the point of view of the killer. I'm sorry to expose you to it, but again, I believe it's integral to understanding the story as a whole.

Now let's hear from Gwen Bishop. Gwen, as I said earlier, was offered the listing on the

Cliff Drive house just three months after Sondra's murder. I interviewed her and have done my best to put her story into an engaging and informative narrative.

1.1.2

IT TOOK Gwen three passes to maneuver her Honda CRV into a tight spot between a MINI and a Ford pickup. Cliff Drive in Laguna Beach bordered Diver's Cove, a popular dive beach in an even more popular tourist town. Parking was at a premium, but that wasn't the only reason it took her so long to settle in and turn off the ignition. Her excitement bordered on anxiety.

"Is this it?" Maricela asked, awe creeping into her tone.

Gwen glanced at the elegant Mediterranean home she'd parked in front of. "No. It's at the end of the block."

She led Maricela up the sandy sidewalk until they reached a fence bulging from a jungle of vines and branches fighting to escape from the yard behind it. All that was visible of the house was a bit of gray, shingled roof rising above the fray.

Gwen pushed open the gate. "This isn't a mini-mansion like the rest of the houses on the street, but, hey, it's beachfront property."

The sound of the gate, hinges half-broken, scraping across the concrete seemed louder than last time she was here. "It's been empty for a long time," she said, then mentally kicked herself. She'd done it again. She was apologizing for the multimillion-dollar property. This house, as dilapidated as it might be, could be a game changer.

"The owner's father died almost a year ago after living in a nursing home for years. She just inherited." Gwen picked her way up the broken walk around the gnarled roots of a large fig tree. Its fruit, in varying stages of decay, littered the ground.

"Do you have the listing already?" Maricela said.

"No, but it's mine if I want it." She spoke slowly, consciously omitting relevant information. Gwen pulled a set of keys from her purse, fitted one into the front door lock and pushed it open. "I need your advice. Fiona, she's the owner, gave me a budget for repairs. It's not big, but it's something."

Gwen squinted into the dim interior, and her heart rate rose. It wasn't only the home's history that caused her reaction. Dark, dank places had always made her nervous, and this house had both. It needed serious help if she was going to move it.

Through the shadows, she could see a circular staircase dividing the foyer in two. A hallway opened to its left. The hallway led to a basement of cave-like rooms. She'd never gone down to see them, and she wasn't planning to. They sounded like a breeding ground for the kind of creepy-crawly things nightmares were made from. Just walking past the cellar door made her queasy.

Milky sunlight beckoned from a room to the right of the stairwell. Gwen hurried toward it. Maricela followed.

"Okay. This is nice." Her friend's voice echoed in the empty living room.

"Nice? It's fantastic." Gwen's tone held a falsely optimistic note. She cleared her throat and walked toward the French doors at the far end of the room. They framed a panoramic view of the Pacific Ocean.

The sight sent a ripple of pleasure up her backbone. It was the primary thing about this house that excited her. Her real estate portfolio to date consisted of tract houses in planned communities, attached townhomes, and condos. Then last week she got the call.

Fiona Randall, a woman she'd sold a three-bedroom to a few years back, had inherited the family home on the cliffs in Laguna Beach. This was the kind of listing that made careers, moved agents out of the scrabbling masses and into the elite ranks of real estate brokers. Gwen had dreamed of breaking into that echelon since she started in the business. However, the house had issues.

She threw open the French doors and stepped onto a veranda of cracked concrete that overlooked a sandy beach. A crisp breeze carried the sounds of crashing waves, children squealing in the surf, and the clanking of diver's equipment. It was a symphony to Gwen's ears.

Yes, this house needed to be renovated and it had baggage. Terrible baggage. But beachfront property in Laguna Beach, California was as rare as red diamonds and much pricier.

"It has beach access." Gwen pointed to a rickety railing rising out of the ice plant at the end of the neglected garden.

Maricela rested a hand on the back of a rusted deck chair, the only piece of furniture on the patio. "If you want to die young."

"It needs a little work." Gwen gestured at the chair and smiled brightly. "That has to go."

"This place needs more than a little work, chica."

"That's why you're here. You're a pro. If you had thirty thousand to throw at it, what would you do?"

Maricela's dark hair reflected the sun as she shook her head. "I'd start by putting a barrier across the top of those stairs. If someone breaks their neck, it'll decrease the value."

Gwen didn't respond. Maricela's joke hit a little too close to the truth for comfort. Instead, she pulled a pad of paper from her purse to make notes.

"Show me more," Maricela said.

Gwen re-entered the gloom of the house and led the way through the living room to the foyer and up the hardwood stairs. "I've been looking at the comps, and nothing with beach access has sold for under twelve million in the past year and a half. Fiona has her hopes set on ten."

Talking about numbers like ten million and twelve million made Gwen feel like a child playing at real estate agent. When she was small, she had a toy cash register on which she rang up plastic food and empty cereal boxes. The prices she set then had no more meaning to her than the price of this house. There were too many zeros for it to compute. But, still, the zeros made her happy.

"Wait until you see the view from the master bedroom," Gwen said.

The floor groaned under their feet as they walked toward a room at the end of the hall. A triangle of light pointed outward from a partially opened door. She looked over her shoulder to monitor Maricela's reaction.

"Ta-da," she said and pushed the door ajar.

Maricela's eyes widened.

"It's spectacular, right?"

Maricela's mouth opened, but she didn't speak.

"You can see Catalina on a clear day." Gwen's voice faltered.

"Oh, chica." Maricela had recognized the room. Gwen could see it on her face. Gruesome photos of what it had once held had been plastered all over the internet. The view, the pale blue walls, and the antique oak bed frame had been visible in many of the shots. "I can't believe you're even thinking about signing this place."

"I'm just considering... I mean..." Gwen stammered.

Maricela turned on her heel and headed toward the stairs. "Murder is a disclosure item," she shot over her shoulder.

1.1.3

FIVE HOURS LATER, Gwen hefted her feet onto the coffee table in her suburban living room and cradled the glass of wine Art had poured for her.

"So, Maricela didn't think you should list the house," he said.

She took a large swig before answering. "No, she didn't, but that was to be expected."

Art sank into his favorite easy chair. It sat across from the couch but was easily angled toward the television. Gwen didn't like the oversized, brown monstrosity. It didn't go with the mid-century modern decor of their home, but it was the only piece of furniture besides their Cal King bed that fit his tall frame. So, she put up with it. Marriage was all about deciding which hills were worth dying on.

"I'm surprised you asked for her opinion." He sipped his own wine, then set it on the coffee table.

Gwen shrugged. She didn't bother explaining that she needed Maricela's expertise. The woman was a force to be reckoned with. She'd won the top agent award at Humboldt Realty the last two years in a row. She had an uncanny ability to know just what alterations a home would need to sell quickly and to sell at the top of the market.

Art gazed at her through blue eyes—sky blue, true blue, trustworthy blue. That was her husband.

He was currently the acting principal of St. Barnabas Lutheran School. At the end of the month, he would be reviewed and either get the job permanently, along with the commensurate raise, or he'd go back to being a lowly English teacher. She had a hard time believing the board wouldn't keep him on. He was made for the job—a cross between pastor and educator. It suited him perfectly.

"I hope she wasn't traumatized," he said.

Gwen rested her head on the couch and stared at the ceiling. "That was over two years ago."

"Yes, but it's the kind of thing you never fully recover— "

"Stop." She held up a hand. "You aren't her psychiatrist, or her priest, or her father. Maricela is a tough lady. She's extremely good at her job, and I need her help."

Art's mouth tightened. "Is she going to give it to you?"

Gwen swung her feet off the table and sat up. "Yes, as a matter of fact, she is. It took some convincing, but she's on board."

"Are you co-listing?"

"No." Neither she nor Maricela wanted that. "I haven't made up my mind about it. She's just giving me some advice—as a friend."

She leaned forward, elbows on her knees, and he leaned back in his chair. It was as if they were on a seesaw, balancing each other while keeping a safe distance. What had happened to them? Three kids? A dog? A mortgage?

"What are you doing tomorrow night?" he asked.

Something warm stirred in Gwen's chest. Maybe she'd pouted too soon. Friday nights used to be reserved for date nights. Was Art reviving the tradition? She smiled. "Why?"

"First school orchestra concert of the semester. They asked me to say a few words before it starts." He lifted his glass from the coffee table and raised it to his mouth. "Thought it would be good to wave the family flag," he said before sipping.

The warm feeling cooled. "I don't know, probably working." Her voice sounded flat, even to her. She stood. "I'd better get dinner going."

"I'll make the salad," he said.

That was Art. Gwen splashed more wine into her glass from the bottle on the kitchen counter. Kind, thoughtful, clean, and thrifty—a regular Boy Scout. Unlike her mother, Gwen had married a good man. However, every once in a while, she wished he'd be bad. Not very bad. Not bad like her father had been, but not quite as perfect.

As she pulled the leftover spaghetti sauce from the fridge and set it on the stove to heat, she allowed her imagination to return to the house on Cliff Drive. She'd made notes of all Maricela's suggestions once she could get her to make them. A vision of clean windows, brightly painted walls, and sunlit rooms now flickered in her mind.

Whatever Art thought, Gwen believed it was good for her friend to face her fears. Wasn't that how people recovered? If you were agoraphobic, you went outside. If you were afraid of snakes, you visited the reptile display at the zoo.

After what had happened in Texas, Maricela had almost quit her job. Instead, she'd gotten counseling, moved to California, and become one of the best real estate agents in Orange County.

Taking her to a home where a crime had been committed was another step toward healing. The murder, just like Maricela's attack, was in the past. Ascribing evil to the places those things had occurred was illogical.

If the property on Cliff Drive were restored, made beautiful again, would anyone remember what had happened there? Didn't the house deserve a second chance?

Art's voice preceded him into the kitchen. "Can you take the kids to school tomorrow?" He entered a second later and gave her an apologetic smile. "Pancake breakfast with the board."

"Sure."

He caught her hand as she turned to the cupboard to get the pasta and pulled her close. "I'm not that worried about Maricela."

"No?" she spoke into his chest.

"No, it's you. I don't like the idea of you listing a house where a woman was stabbed to death."

"That was three months ago."

"I know, but..." Instead of finishing his sentence, he pressed his lips to the top of her head for a long minute, then released her.

"When's dinner? I'm starving." Tyler, their eleven-year-old, burst into the kitchen through the back door.

"Ten minutes," Gwen said.

He turned and yelled into the yard. "Ten minutes." Then, he disappeared again.

Gwen and Art worked together to get dinner on the table as they'd done a thousand times before. Their conversation turned to school gossip and Art's mother's health.

It wasn't exciting or passionate, like in the early days of their marriage. It was more like a well-rehearsed scene from a beloved movie. The ending might not be a surprise, but it was still enjoyable to watch it play out. She and Art were a team. They were good together, and that was enough for now.

1.1.4

GWEN TAPPED out her frustration on the steering wheel. "What is going on up there? You'd think they were being dropped off for a six-month tour with the Peace Corps instead of six hours of school."

The twice-daily traffic jam at St. Barnabas Lutheran School reminded her of a herd of cattle headed for a watering hole. Mothers in minivans rattled their horns and jostled each other to best position their young.

"Everyone have their backpacks? Lunch?" Gwen said when she was able to pull the CRV forward.

"Keep driving, Mom," Tyler said. "We'll jump and roll." Tyler was the funny man in the family.

Emily, the youngest, not to be outdone by her older brothers, said, "Yeah, let's jump and roll."

"You'll mess up your uniform," Gwen said.

She jockeyed left to the drop-off point. Tyler and Emily bolted from the seat behind her, and Jason, her oldest, exited the shotgun position.

"You have your sister," Gwen said when Jason came around the driver's side. "Take her to her classroom, please." Jason gave her a quizzical look. Emily was in third grade and had been walking to her class alone all school year.

"Or, not," Gwen amended. She was being twitchy—had been all

week as Art had pointed out last night. He thought she was nervous about the Laguna Beach listing. He was wrong. She didn't know what it was, but it wasn't that. There was no reason to be twitchy about that.

Her children turned to walk toward the brick front building.

"Hey. Goodbye." She called after them.

Emily returned, stood on tiptoes, wrapped her arms around Gwen's neck and leaned in for a sticky kiss. Tyler, smelling like soap and cereal, was next. Jason stooped; the top of his red head entered the window first. He pecked her on the cheek. When had he gotten so tall?

Then they were off. Jason loped with the awkward gait of a teen whose brain hasn't figured out how to handle the extra inches. The two towheads jogged to keep up with him. Gwen watched until they reached the double glass doors of the school, love making her heart ache. A horn behind her sounded, reminding her of the day ahead. She put the car in gear.

This morning, she was meeting Fiona Randall and a contractor at the Laguna Beach house. Fiona had called to ask if they could all get together to discuss what needed to be done to get the place ready to sell.

It had only been available for a week when Sondra Olsen of First Team Realty had been found in the master bedroom. The police believed she'd been killed in the basement, then carried upstairs and arranged on the rug near the bed.

The story had received a lot of media attention. It was sensational—realtor dies in multimillion-dollar beach house. Time and a flood of other horrid news stories were the only things that would dim the community's memory of the crime. Hopefully, enough of both had flowed by.

Fiona and a tall, dark-haired man were already there when Gwen arrived on Cliff Drive. They stood in a patch of sunlight next to the creaky gate, their backs to the street. Fiona waved at the fig tree while the man nodded. Gwen hoped she was giving orders to have the eyesore removed.

She parked, exited her car, and clicked the locks shut. Fiona and the man turned at the sound. "Hi, sorry I'm late." She began making excuses as she crossed the street.

"You're not," Fiona reassured her.

The man held out his hand. "Lance."

She took it and gazed at his face. It was a very nice face. Too nice, really. He was the kind of handsome she often took an instant dislike to. The entitled kind of handsome. The kind of handsome that produced shallow people who'd never had to endure the slings and arrows everyone else had to endure.

"Gwen." She shook the proffered hand.

A comical expression crossed Lance's face as he looked from one to the other of the women. "Are you two sisters?"

Fiona grinned. "No. We should be though."

"You look so much alike."

Lance wasn't the first to note the similarity in their appearances. Although there was a superficial resemblance between them—they were both tall with lean builds—their faces weren't the same at all. An observant person would notice that Gwen's features were much larger than Fiona's patrician ones.

What caused the comments was their unusual hair color. Each had a head of thick, wavy, auburn hair and they wore it in the same casual, mid-length cut. Gwen was thinking of cutting hers.

"Were you a carrot top when you were a kid?" Fiona asked.

"I was. I hated my hair."

"Me, too."

"Well, the pain paid off," Lance said, with inappropriate admiration in his voice.

"What were you two talking about when I pulled up?" Gwen gestured to the fig tree, wanting to change the subject. Her hair was none of Lance's business. "Getting rid of that, I hope."

"Yes," Fiona said. "I was telling him how it blocks the light in the entryway."

"Can we take a look?" he said.

As they walked through the home, Gwen laid out the suggestions Maricela had made about bathroom upgrades, new windows, and brighter colors on the walls. It sounded as if she'd already made up her mind to list the property, which she hadn't, but the idea of renovating the old place was exciting. She'd love to watch it transform into a more modern version of its original elegant form.

Fiona nodded her agreement as Gwen spoke, but Lance only jotted notes into a tablet. Gwen tried, unsuccessfully, to read them over his shoulder. What did he think of her ideas? Well, of Maricela's ideas. And why was he being so quiet? And why did she care?

When they came to the kitchen, he finally spoke up. "This is a mess."

"It needs new appliances," Gwen said, a little defensively.

"Needs a lot more than appliances." He walked to the sink and turned on the tap. A loud bang sounded from someplace inside the walls. Fifteen seconds later, water spit from the faucet.

"I'd suggest having a plumber in to look at the pipes. It'd be a shame to have to pull up the new flooring if you got a leak," he said.

"Who says we're putting in new flooring?" Gwen stomped her foot on the boards. "This is hardwood."

Lance crossed to the butler's pantry, bent down, and pulled up a section of the floor before she could protest. "The kitchen needs tile." He carried it to the women with arms extended, like it might explode.

The smell made her wince. It was green with mold. "Future health hazard," he said.

Fiona grimaced. "I may have to increase the budget."

Lance dropped the wood, wiped his hands on his pants, turned to his tablet on the counter and began scrolling through a very thorough-looking form. It seemed to cover all the things they'd discussed, including costs and time estimates.

Gwen wandered away as the two pored over the document. She needed a moment to think. She opened the French doors and walked onto the balcony, breathing in salt air to wash imagined mold spores from her lungs.

Did she or didn't she plan to represent Fiona Randall? She was torn. The house was in terrible condition, but the woman was obviously willing to invest in improvements. She'd hired a contractor.

No, the real reason Gwen was hesitant was because of the murder, which was completely illogical. As she'd said to Maricela and to Art, she didn't believe there was such a thing as resident evil. She couldn't accept that the violence done here had somehow permeated the walls. That, like blood spatter that had been scrubbed away, it would reappear if the conditions were right.

"Gwen?" Fiona's voice echoed from the empty living room. "Here." Gwen turned toward the sound.

A moment later the homeowner stepped onto the patio, Lance directly behind her. "Needs paving." He made an adjustment on his tablet.

Fiona's face clouded. "I hate to put my entire inheritance into fixing this place."

"You'll get it all back and then some when it sells," Lance said.

"If it sells," she said.

Gwen took a step toward her. "It will. This is Laguna Beach."

"I'm tempted to put it up 'as is' again."

"That's not—"

"I wouldn't—"

Lance and Gwen both spoke at once. She closed her mouth and let him continue.

"The place is one of a kind. Make it shine, and you can ask whatever you want."

Fiona massaged her forehead as if she were struggling with a headache. "It's one of a kind, alright."

Gwen felt a surge of sympathy. The house was both a gift and a burden, one she may be able to help carry. "I agree with Lance," she added quickly. "You can't erase the home's past, but you could disguise it."

Fiona's hand slapped to her side, and she glared at Gwen. "You know we're going to have lookie-loos from all over the county here as soon as we put it on the market."

Gwen inclined her head. "All the more reason to manage perceptions."

Lance's brow furrowed. "What are you talking about?" Both women's eyes shot toward him.

"You don't know?" Fiona asked.

"Know what?"

She bit her bottom lip as if she hated to tell him.

Gwen did it for her. "The first real estate agent to list the property was found dead—stabbed—in an upstairs bedroom three months ago."

Lance took a step backward, as if he'd been pushed. "What?"

"Some days I feel I'm responsible. That this house..." Fiona reached an icy hand toward Gwen and gripped her wrist. "Maybe I shouldn't list it again."

The thought that she could become a target had never occurred to Gwen. It chilled her as much as Fiona's touch.

Lance blinked hard. "Do they know who did it?"

Fiona shook her head slowly. "No. At first, they thought it was the husband. They'd been having troubles. But he had an alibi."

"It was probably random, like what happened in Texas a couple of years ago," Gwen blurted.

Lance turned a blank gaze on her.

"Real estate agents were being attacked in vacant properties." Maricela's face appeared in Gwen's mind. "It was terrible. They never caught the guy."

"The victims were raped, not killed," Fiona amended.

"This could've been a copycat that went wrong," Gwen said. "Or maybe it was a lover, or an angry co-worker. We don't know who killed Sondra, but there's no reason to think this house—" She lifted her hands and gestured around her. "Had anything to do with it."

Nobody spoke for a long minute. The waves crashing on the shore below filled the silence. Finally, Lance said, "I'll write this up and send you over a contract tomorrow. If you want to go forward, I can get started on Monday. I had a cancellation."

He nodded goodbye and left. Fiona watched him go, then looked at Gwen. "You never sent me a listing agreement."

"I know. Things at work..." She allowed her excuse to trail off. She didn't want to tell Fiona she hadn't made up her mind. Why wouldn't she jump at the chance to add this house to her portfolio? Superstition and fear, those were the only reasons.

The same superstition and fear plagued Fiona, however, and she seemed to understand. "You saw the lockbox on the front door?"

Gwen nodded.

"I'm leaving it for the workmen, but you still have the keys I gave you, right?"

She did. The fact that she hadn't brought them, hadn't returned them, said something. Gwen was leaning toward taking the listing.

Fiona touched her arm lightly. "Feel free to come by, walk around, think about it."

"I will." Relieved the conversation was over, Gwen moved toward the house.

"But, Gwen," Fiona said.

Gwen turned.

"I need to know by Monday. Other agents have contacted me." She raised a hand, palm forward in a gesture of peace. "I'm not pushing. You know that. But I need someone to oversee the renovations. I've got too much going on to do it myself."

"Of course," Gwen said.

"I hope it will be you." She lifted a lock of hair. "Sisters and all."

Gwen grinned. "I'm sure it will be. I just have to look at the schedule."

It should be her. When she was on the veranda looking at the ocean view, she felt confident. But as she passed the cellar door in the dim front hall, an involuntary shiver walked up her spine, and the confidence fled.

1.1.5

THAT NIGHT, Gwen sat with Maricela in the neighborhood wine bar. They were swapping stories and sipping wine with some of the other agents from the office.

"So, wait, you were going to hit him over the head with a lamp?" Maricela asked, eyes wide over her wine glass.

"It was all I could find," Gwen said. "I almost fainted. I was so relieved when I saw a tape measure come out of his pocket."

It was happy hour at The Leaky Barrel, a wine shop and tasting room a few doors down from the office. It wasn't the most elegant spot in town—too dark and dim. It had been decorated to look like an old sailing vessel. Everything was lined with wood: wood shelving, wood floors, wood paneling on the little bit of wall visible between bottles.

Gwen half-expected to feel the sway of waves beneath her feet when she stepped through the doorway. After a few glasses of wine, the illusion was known to cause seasickness. But it was convenient, and it was a Friday night tradition.

"What did he say? He liked your butt?" Carolyn, another woman from the office, had squeezed up to the table next to Maricela.

"No, I thought that's what he meant though. He said—" Gwen lowered her voice in a fair imitation of her now infamous ex-client, Arnold Paul. "'I like backsides.'"

"Backsides?" Maricela looked confused.

"He meant he liked bedrooms that faced the backyard, but I thought—"

A loud gong announced Donald Gordon's entrance. A ship's bell—large and brass and covered in a green patina as if it had been exposed to the elements for years—was affixed to the front door of the shop. It was another affectation; one Gwen found annoying.

Don walked across the weathered floorboards toward the women like an aging Shakespearean actor on a stage. "What's so funny?" He glanced at their smiling faces.

Most of the regulars from the office had filtered into the Barrel between 5:00 and 5:30 to enjoy their TGIF celebration. It was now quarter past six, and their first glasses of wine had taken effect. Camaraderie flowed like the libations. The week's victory stories were more impressive, and the jokes were funnier. Humboldt agents had become "us," their clients, "them." Gwen wondered why she hadn't done this more often.

"Gwen thought her client was coming on to her," Maricela said in an unamused voice.

"But it turns out he just wanted to measure her hips." Carolyn giggled, making the décolletage peeking out from her fuzzy pink sweater wobble. Carolyn was forty-ish, single, and dressed for maximum attention, leopard print pumps and all.

One-half of Don's mouth turned up, and he raised his eyebrows at Gwen.

"It was nothing," she said. "That Chicago couple I was carting around last month wanted to see one of my listings, but only the husband showed up. I let my imagination run away with me."

"Wait a minute," Don said and raised a finger to summon the proprietor. "What happened to the buddy system?"

When Maricela joined Humboldt, she brought the concept of a buddy system with her. Texas real estate companies had instituted it when the attacks were occurring, but it never really caught on in California. Don was teasing Gwen, but Maricela took him seriously.

"Really—" Gwen started to say.

"Gwen is too focused on the deal," Maricela said. She spoke like

Gwen wasn't sitting there right next to her. It was annoying. "She's like my daughter, Julissa," Maricela continued. "Cares too much what other people think. But, Julissa has an excuse. She's fifteen, not almost—"

"What was I supposed to do?" Gwen interrupted before Maricela mentioned her age. A vanity maybe, but she was feeling self-conscious about her fortieth right around the corner. "The client was at my elbow the entire time. And he was very sensitive—a real chip on his shoulder. I couldn't exactly make him wait until someone from the office showed up to chaperone."

"Mo, can I have another merlot please," Carolyn said when the wine shop owner came over with Don's glass.

"And are we having the Braided Vine or the Adele Cellar?" he asked.

"I had the Braided, but which do you like best?" Carolyn fluttered her eyelashes. Mo sniffed and pulled out the Adele Cellar.

Carolyn was interested, Gwen thought with amusement. But why not? She and the proprietor looked to be about the same age. Gwen wondered what he'd look like without the omnipresent ship captain's cap he wore. His features were nice enough. He wasn't her type, but he had a refined way about him she imagined was attractive to some.

"I put an app on Julissa's phone," Maricela told Don. "I know where she is at all times. She doesn't want to check in with me in front of the other kids, so that's what she gets."

"Ooh, I should get that app." Carolyn's expression went from excited to depressed in three seconds flat. "But who'd care where I was?"

"So it works? You can keep track of her?" Don leaned over Maricela's phone, and she showed him the features. He didn't care about it. He was flirting.

His profile was still strong and chiseled. It reminded Gwen of a Greek bust she'd seen at the Getty Museum. If she were a director, she'd cast him as an aging Caesar, or Pericles. But however well preserved he was, he was still too old for Maricela.

He glanced at Gwen as if he could feel her eyes on him. She jumped up and walked to the bar. She didn't want to talk to him. Mo acknowledged her with a nod, and she ordered more Cabernet.

She hadn't been planning to have another, but it was the first deflection that came to mind. Don had been trying to sidle up to her ever since she'd mentioned she might be taking the listing in Laguna. She'd been doing her best to avoid him.

Mo filled her glass, and she took a sip. Now she would have to stay, not only until it was drunk, but also until she wasn't.

It didn't matter, though. Art wasn't going to be home until late. He and the kids were going to the school concert, then out for pizza. Gwen felt a little guilty she hadn't attended, but she'd promised Maricela she'd meet her for a glass of wine. Besides, she was making a point by her absence.

If Art wanted to be *el presidente* of St. Barnabas, God bless him. She didn't plan to be *la primera dama*. Her mother had been her father's wingman, the wind beneath his wings, his guardian angel, whatever. He'd had many names for her. All lovely. But none of them stopped him from abandoning her when a younger cherub flew into his life. Art would have to accept that he and she were a team with different, but equal, roles.

"So you were almost strangled with a tape measure." A warm voice close to her ear startled her. "That seems a fitting death for a realtor." Don sat on the stool next to her.

She exhaled with frustration but pasted on a smile. "Better for an interior designer."

"True." He nodded. "I guess if I were going to kill an agent, I'd suffocate her under a mountain of paperwork."

"You got that right."

"So I heard a rumor that you're about to sign that Laguna Beach house where the agent was killed." Don twirled the stem of his glass and adopted a casual tone, but Gwen heard the steel in his voice.

"I am," she said simply. Fiona's words, other agents have contacted me, rang through her mind. She wouldn't be surprised if Don was one of them.

"Sure you're not opening Pandora's box?"

"How so?" She knew what he meant, but didn't want to play his game. Don was well off. He'd had a long and successful career, but he wasn't ready to throw in the towel. He had something to prove. Maybe he was overcompensating because his wife left him a few years back for another man, she didn't know, but his competitive spirit bordered on cutthroat.

"It could be a media nightmare. You know, murder house on the market again, yada, yada, yada."

"Well, you know what they say about publicity," Gwen said.

"Yeah, it's all good." He waved a dismissive hand. "Don't you believe it. People don't move into haunted houses."

She begged to differ with him. The Amityville Horror house had been occupied by living humans for decades. She kept her thoughts to herself, though.

A bubble of laughter burst at the high-top table where the Humboldt agents sat. Gwen slid off her stool. "Who says it's haunted?"

He blinked at her as if in surprise. "I heard one of those ghoul-hunting TV shows was trying to get in for the night."

Fiona hadn't said anything about that, but Gwen was sure she wouldn't allow it. "I don't believe in ghosts."

"All I'm saying is if you feel the need for help from someone older and wiser, someone who's been around the block a few times, I'm at your service."

"Thanks, Don." *In your dreams,* she added silently and wandered toward her other co-workers.

"So, I shove the panties under the bed with my foot while I try to distract my client with the view out the bedroom window, which, believe me, is nothing to write home about. I think she thought I was a nut case," Carolyn said.

Maricela and two other women from the office laughed.

"You should have seen the backyard of the house I showed two weeks ago," Maricela said. "I never take people to a house I haven't previewed, but I had a busy week, and... well, anyway, the whole yard was covered in pink flamingos and dog crap. *Qué lío.* The lady of the house had four Chihuahuas. She said the flamingos were there to keep them company."

The-worst-thing-I've-ever-seen-in-a-house was a popular game among real estate agents. Gallows humor helped release the tension from what could be an unnerving job at times. Gwen often had to override her own common sense.

Even her kids knew it was stupid to go into unoccupied houses with people they didn't know. She'd warned them about stranger danger from the time they could talk. Never take candy from strangers, or help a guy in a van find a puppy, or go anywhere with anyone who didn't know the secret password.

Now here she was at almost forty doing her best to ignore the red flags she taught them to heed, to discount the very rules her parents had inculcated into her. And she wasn't the only one. Every agent she knew, especially the females, felt the same tremors.

"The most terrible experience I ever had, hands down, was the cockroach house," Carolyn said, and smiled at Mo as he handed her another glass of wine. She was on a roll.

"You win." Gwen groaned and placed her hands over her ears. "Please don't tell that story again. I don't even like to think about it."

"That's right, you're cockroach-phobic," Carolyn said, pretending she'd totally forgotten. "Tell you what, I won't talk about it if you cover my bar tab." She smiled sweetly.

"I haven't heard it." Don Gordon had returned to the group behind Gwen. "How do I know if it's worse than the panties if I don't get to hear it?"

"Trust me," Gwen said. "It's worse than a pair of panties on the floor."

"They weren't clean," Carolyn said.

"Yuck, and it's still worse."

"Carolyn's on her third glass of wine. That's a lot of money to cough up," Don said.

"Third and last," she said. "It's almost closing time."

"Cockroaches?" Don said.

Gwen downed the last of her drink and headed out the door. She'd be damned if she'd listen to that story again.

MOLLY: I completely relate to Gwen. I hate cockroaches too.

But on the bigger issue, what do you think? Will she take the listing or not? Better yet, do you think she should take the listing? Why? Why not?

Let's talk about it on Facebook. Follow the link in the show notes for the group page.

(cue music)

VO: If you enjoyed this episode, please leave us a five-star review on your favorite podcast service—it really helps. *Murders Under the Sun* is edited by Jim Wilbourne, theme music is by Eclectic Blends, and I'm your host, Molly Shure.

part three

MURDERS UNDER THE SUN
SEASON ONE; EPISODE TWO

MOLLY: Welcome back to *Murders Under the Sun*. I'm Molly Shure, your host.

In episode one of *The Cliff House*, we met the cast of characters impacted by the Real Estate Killer's crimes. I don't know about you, but the journal entry at the beginning of the episode made me shiver.

We also heard from Gwen Bishop, an agent who was offered a listing on the cliff house only three months after Sondra's brutal murder. Gwen's hesitation to list the property where a killing was committed—her inner conflict—was very apparent.

Thank you to everyone who left comments on social media. I love reading your thoughts. It helps me know you're out there, and I'm not just speaking into the void.

The humor was appreciated too. Most of you said either: She should take the listing or we won't have much of a show. Or she will take the listing for the same reason. I will try to make the questions of the week a little more provocative in the future. But moving along…

In this episode, we'll find out how Gwen justified her decision. Since you all guessed that's what would happen, I'm not spoiling anything by telling you up front that she did.

We'll also meet two new individuals, Brian McKibben and his mother Olivia Richards. Although their story may seem tangential, it's important.

Remember, in the introduction to the season I mentioned that the primary connection I saw

between this series of crimes wasn't the criminals, but the victims. Strangely enough, Brian
and Olivia will move to center stage in Season
Two of the podcast, which I'll be calling *The
Garden*.

But, let's not jump ahead of ourselves. Again,
I'm beginning the episode with a word from REK—
aka the Real Estate Killer.

1.2.2

I PULLED the wrinkled newspaper article from my drawer and stared at it as I had almost weekly for the past few months. It was illogical, but I hoped that if I looked long and hard enough, the answer to my dilemma would leap from the page into my consciousness.

But I saw what I'd seen a hundred times before, a color photograph of the house with yellow crime scene tape encircling it like a ribbon around a gift. I had handed it to the police. Made a present of it. At the time, it had galled me I'd been so short-sighted.

I could have disposed of Sondra's body anywhere, but no. I left her in the very place I least wanted to call attention to. Well, almost. I'd taken her upstairs. I would no more have sullied that cellar than Howard Carter would have urinated in King Tut's tomb. But, still, I might as well have stood on the roof of the house with a megaphone and barked, "Step right up, gentlemen." I'd made a circus of the place.

The only excuse I can offer is that I was beside myself. It was, after all, a very eventful day. I'd scaled the castle wall for the first time, killed a gorgon, and found a treasure. Lesser deeds have had entire tomes written about them. Nevertheless, the house crawled with police for weeks. They'd swarmed in like cockroaches, invading every corner. They were looking for clues to Sondra's killer, clues they weren't going to find. I'd been careful about that. But the fact they were there at all had worried me. There were other things they could have found.

Time had passed, however, and nothing more had happened. I thought perhaps my mistake worked out for the best. After all, who would want to purchase a house where a murder has been committed? I'd allowed myself to hope that Fiona would let the place lie, abandon the idea of selling for the foreseeable future. At least, until I could come up with a plan to make the house mine.

It should have been mine by rights. When the old man died, he should have left it to me. I spoke to a lawyer about it, but he said I didn't have a case. What does he know?

A month after the police tape came down, I found I couldn't stay away. I wanted—no, needed—to be close to my treasure. As dangerous as it sounds, I moved in.

Oh, not full time. I had to work, and coming and going every day would've been sure to attract attention no matter how careful I was. No, I only went on weekends.

Every Friday night for the past two months, I've packed an overnight bag, a few provisions, a good book or two, and headed to my beach house. I spend my time wandering the rooms, sitting in the sun on the sheltered veranda, and sleeping in my father's bed. These weekends have been a solace to my wounded soul.

Then last Friday, the unthinkable happened. I found a lockbox on the front door. Fiona, the idiot, must be planning to sell the place again. It didn't deter me from spending the weekend. I never enter through the front door, anyway, but it was worrisome.

I turned my focus to the paper in my hands again, willing something to bleed from the page into my mind. I was about to give up, fold it, and stick it away when, all at once, a line I'd read more times than I can count changed. It morphed from normal newspaper font to bold, neon letters right before my eyes. The words screamed from the page. I couldn't believe I hadn't seen them sooner.

INVESTIGATORS on the scene had no comment when asked if they believed the crime was related to the attacks committed against Texas real estate agents in recent years.

The investigators had no comment. What did no comment always mean? It meant there were many comments on the topic when no reporters were within shouting distance. It meant they were halfway convinced the statement was true, but they didn't have evidence to support their suspicions.

I saw an opportunity. I would give them the substantiation they desired. I'd been so preoccupied with trying to protect what was mine, I'd overlooked the obvious. A copycat crime was the perfect solution.

The Texas housing market had tanked in the cities where the attacks had taken place, and those crimes were mere rapes, not murders. Rape, to my mind, was both distasteful and showed a certain lack of self-control. I would do better than that. I had done better. Let them think the Texas rapist had graduated to greater crimes. I only hoped the actual culprit didn't come hunting me for plagiarism.

Yes, the best way to keep my house from selling was to make it unsaleable. If one corpse took it off the market for three months, what would two do?

If the next real estate agent who brought a buyer to the table ended up six feet under, well, that would be a deterrent. Wouldn't it?

A serious deterrent. But hopefully, it wouldn't come to that. I was sure I could come up with other ways to make the place unattractive.

Cheered, I refolded the newspaper clipping and shoved it into my drawer. Next on the agenda, find some way to keep up with the doings on Cliff Drive. I hummed a tune from my childhood as I typed "listening devices" into the search engine of my computer.

1.2.3

MOLLY: I imagine you can guess what REK does next. But poor Gwen had no idea. As we continue the story from her viewpoint, you'll see that she is completely in the dark. She had no way of knowing that the Real Estate Killer still had access to the property and no way of knowing that he was planning to keep an eye—or an ear—on her.

But, enough of me. Let's let Gwen tell her story.

Gwen slipped off her shoes as she entered her house, then picked them up by their straps. She'd been in heels all day. The hardwood floor felt cool and lovely against her feet.

She heard the click of dog paws, and a second later, Rocket, their black lab mix, rounded the corner to greet her. "Hey, boy." She scratched his ears with her free hand as he nuzzled her leg with a damp nose.

"Gwen?" Art called from the living room.

She padded toward his voice. Rocket followed. Art sat in his old leather chair, remote in hand and TV on mute. Gwen planted a kiss on top of his head and sank onto the couch. "How was the concert?"

"Fine." But he didn't look as though it had been fine. His face was pinched, his eyes hooded and dark.

A niggle of worry broke through Gwen's happy wine haze. "What happened?"

Art closed his eyes as if gathering his thoughts. "We went to Enzo's for pizza after the concert," he finally said.

Gwen waited.

"Carrie Sherman." He opened his eyes and gazed at her. "You remember her?"

Gwen nodded slowly. "She was in your AP English a couple of years ago, wasn't she? Wrote that funny story about her dog getting into the neighbor's trash?"

"Right. Good memory. She was our server."

"I didn't know she worked at Enzo's." And it didn't matter, did it? There was something upsetting Art, and she didn't think it had anything to do with Carrie Sherman's job history. When Art was upset, Gwen got upset. It was a spousal thing. She was babbling.

"She does, but..." He paused. "Doesn't matter. Anyway, Carrie comes over to take our order. I ask her how everything is going. She says they're having a rough night because everyone is worried."

"Why are they worried?" Gwen asked.

"She said it as if I ought to know why."

"But you didn't?"

"No." Art shook his head. "I had no idea."

Impatience joined the uneasiness in Gwen's chest. "What was it?"

"Brian McKibben—he's in the third grade—was hit by a truck this afternoon."

"Oh, no. Art. Is he...?"

Art waved a hand. "No. No, he's not dead. He is in a coma, though."

Gwen felt a small relief, very small. "That's terrible. Every parent's nightmare."

"It was a hit and run."

"Who would do a thing like that?"

Art leaned forward, picked up a bottle from the floor near his chair, and added a splash of whiskey to a tumbler that sat on the coffee table. Gwen hadn't noticed either the bottle or the glass. Seeing them made her unease grow.

Her husband wasn't a drinker. He'd have a glass or two of wine with her on weekends or special occasions, but the whiskey was reserved for guests and hot toddies during flu season. As upsetting as the story was, there must be more to it. Art was taking it personally.

"His mother, Olivia Richards, is single. She works at Enzo's. That's how Carrie knew."

It struck Gwen that the mother and son's last names were different. "His father?"

"Drinking problem. They're either separated or divorced." Art took an ironic swig of whiskey. "Not in the picture. Brian is a scholarship student."

The story was tragic. A struggling single mother. Her son in a coma after a hit-and-run. The wayward father. It had all the elements of a TV drama. But that didn't explain the grief and guilt written all over Art's face. These people weren't family. They weren't even friends.

"There's more?" she asked.

Art winced as if in pain. "It's my fault."

For a crazy moment Gwen thought Art might be the driver who'd hit Brian. That he'd been at that whiskey all afternoon, had taken out the car, and plowed into the poor kid.

But no. Art wouldn't do a thing like that and, if he did, he'd never run. He took responsibility for his actions. He was the most responsible person Gwen knew. "How could that be?"

His gazed shot toward her. "I suspended him for the week, beginning Monday."

She was confused. "So? I don't see how—"

Art cut her off. "He was home alone. His mother had to work." He took another gulp of whiskey.

"And?"

"And." His voice was sharp. "He was home alone. He went out skateboarding."

"He was skateboarding?"

"That's what I just said."

"But how is this your fault?" Gwen spread her hands, a pleading gesture. "Kids skateboard all the time. Our kids skateboard."

Art leaned toward her. "Olivia told him not to skateboard on the road. It's dangerous."

"He disobeyed. Kids dis—"

"Olivia's shifts are during school hours," he interrupted her again. "She schedules them that way so that she can be there when Brian gets home, but Brian was suspended."

Understanding dawned. Art was taking responsibility for Brian's bad behavior. Bad behavior that landed him in the hospital. "Oh, Art. You can't."

He tipped his head to one side. "Can't what?"

"You can't make this about you." Gwen leaned toward him and, for once, he didn't lean away. "I'm sure he deserved to be suspended or you wouldn't have done it. You don't have a crystal ball. You couldn't know that he would have an accident."

"I should've given him detention. That way he'd have been locked up safe and sound all afternoon, but I thought—" He waved his tumbler. "I thought it would be a hardship for his mother to have to race over after work to pick him up by 5:00."

Gwen lifted her palms toward him. "Exactly. You were trying to do the right thing. You can't blame yourself."

He was quiet for a long moment. So long, Gwen wondered if he'd drunk enough to pass out. When he spoke, she jumped. "Whether I blame myself or not—which I do, emphatically and wholeheartedly— the board will blame me."

A chilly breeze blew through the front window. Gwen crossed the room and closed it, but didn't return to the couch. Instead, she walked to the cold fireplace and leaned against the mantle. "How could they?"

"I should've realized a single mother can't manage a radical shift in her schedule like that. My actions will be seen as out of touch. We—" He gestured to her and back to himself with his glass. "We are rich and privileged."

"But we're not..." Gwen started to protest, then clamped her mouth shut. Rich was subjective. Compared to Fiona and her multimillion-dollar inheritance, they weren't rich. Compared to a single mother working in an Italian diner and living in a rental, they were loaded. Art was right.

"I don't know which is worse, that I suspended Brian, or that I care what the board thinks. The poor kid is in the hospital fighting for his life, and I'm worried about my job." He set the glass on the coffee table and dropped his head into his hands.

Gwen moved to his chair, perched on its arm, and wrapped her arms around him. She shared some of his guilt, because she was worried about his position at the school, as well. Did that make them bad people? "We'll figure this out."

"I can tell you; I'm going to do whatever I can to help Olivia Richards," he said.

That should have comforted Gwen, but it didn't. It proved what she already knew, that her husband was a good man, an upright man. Yet, although she couldn't say why, something in his statement filled her with dread.

1.2.4

MONDAY CAME without its usual slump. Gwen watched Art and the kids drive away from the house with relief. The weekend had been exhausting. She and Art had juggled events and chores like they were flaming torches. They'd managed to maintain the status quo when the kids were watching, but just.

They'd cheered at Tyler's Little League game, oohed and aahed at the cupcakes Emily had decorated at a friend's birthday party, and reminded Jason three times to do his history paper. But they were only going through the motions. Whenever the kids were out of the room, the conversation returned to Brian and his mother like a boomerang.

Art had slipped off to the hospital on Saturday afternoon and come home in an even darker mood. Brian's brain was swollen. The doctors had put him into a drug-induced coma. They didn't want to run the risk that he might wake, but no one would know the extent of the damage until he did. Olivia was distraught and hadn't left his side. It was a nightmare.

Sunday hadn't been any better. They'd prayed for Brian at church, but even that didn't lift the gloom that hovered over their household. For once, work seemed like a respite.

Gwen cleared up the breakfast things, dressed in jeans and a blouse, and headed to Laguna, grateful for a project that would take her mind off things at home. She parked behind a large, expensive-looking pickup truck that probably belonged to Lance.

He was meeting with a plumber at 9:00. She planned to do one more walkthrough, talk with Lance about his timetable, and return to the office to write up a contract. After learning that Art may no longer be in the running for the principal position at St. Barnabas, she didn't see how she could refuse to list the property. Their family needed the money, and there was no logical reason not to.

Gwen put a hand on the old gate, ready to give it shove, but it flew forward without any pressure. Lance must not have closed it all the way. The front door was slightly ajar as well.

She called to him as she entered, but he didn't answer. "Lance," she called again, but the only sound she heard was the click of her sandals on the wood flooring. Gwen walked past the stairs and into the living room. It was empty.

She circled through the dining room and into the kitchen, dropping her purse on the counter as she walked through. Lance wasn't in either of those rooms. She checked the downstairs office and bathroom. They were vacant as well. Could it be the truck she'd parked behind belonged to someone else? But, if it wasn't his, who'd let themself into the house?

Gwen returned to the foyer, more uneasy than she'd been when she'd entered. She glanced at the staircase. He could be on the second floor. Correction, whoever had left the front door ajar could be on the second floor. She should go up and investigate, but a frisson of nerves washed over her.

She bristled at her body's reaction to the situation. This was stupid. If she were going to represent Fiona, she couldn't slink around the property like a skittish cat.

As she placed a foot on the bottom stair, her gaze fell on the door to the basement. It was also open. Her heart danced in her chest, but she strode toward the cellar entrance with deliberate steps.

She hadn't been downstairs but had heard it held many rooms filled with detritus of the past. Apparently, Fiona's father had only gotten around to clearing one or two of them since he'd never needed the space. Perhaps Lance went down to investigate. They'd need to clean everything out.

The light switch on the wall just inside the doorway had been toggled on. Gwen could see the first three in what she assumed was a long series of yellow bulbs hanging from the ceiling. The stairs had once been painted green but were now chipped and stained with age. She was surprised Lance had trusted his weight on them. They were broken in places, and even the boards that remained intact looked rickety.

She leaned through the doorway as far as she dared. "Lance," she called. Nothing. Then, louder. "Lance?"

"Hello." A faint voice floated from the dim space below. "Be up in a second."

"I'll make coffee," she shouted. Mystery solved. As she stepped away from the basement, an excessive sense of relief washed over her. Gwen wished the home was cellar-free like the vast majority of Southern California houses. There were many things about this house she'd change if she could.

She walked out front, enjoying the feel of the sunshine on her skin more than usual. Even her car was warm to the touch as she popped her trunk hatch and lifted out her open-house box. It would be a perfect day to sit on a blanket at the beach. Gwen raised her face to the sky, inhaled the sea air, then trudged into the house again.

By the time she returned to the house with the box, Lance was standing in the foyer, clapping dust off his hands. "So dirty."

"You wouldn't catch me down there."

"You haven't been?" he asked.

"No." She said the word with finality and didn't elaborate. He made a sound that might've been surprise. She ignored it, headed to the kitchen, and dropped the box on the counter.

Lance followed behind her. "You're not curious? There might be hidden treasure."

Gwen began unpacking the box, pulling out the coffee pot, coffee and creamer cups, sugar packets, a box of cookies, and scented candles. "No treasure is worth risking my life on those stairs."

"This from the woman who was so excited about the beach access." Hope you don't need special water for this pot."

"Tap is okay, as long as it's not rusty or anything."

"Not rusty."

They chatted about the plumbing and made coffee. As Gwen took her first sip, a cranky-sounding doorbell rang.

"Ah, the man of the hour has arrived." Lance went to answer the door. A moment later, he returned with a short, round man in a blue uniform.

Gwen followed them through the downstairs, listening in on their conversation long enough to feel confident that Lance knew his job and had Fiona's best interests at heart. Maybe he wasn't as bad as she'd assumed. Looks could be deceiving.

She returned to the kitchen, fished a measuring tape and a pad of paper from her purse, then headed up the stairs, leaving the men on the main floor. Early morning sunlight spilled into the hallway from the bedrooms at the front of the house.

Why not start there and avoid the master bedroom for a few more minutes? She shut down the thought. The master bedroom had been sanitized by a professional team after the murder. There was nothing there to worry about.

Gwen entered one of the smaller bedrooms and walked across to the window. A layer of dust covered the sill. She made a memo to book cleaning services when the renovations were nearing completion. She measured the square footage and made notes about the closets.

After she repeated the process in the second bedroom, she left the brightly lit front rooms and walked into the dimness at the rear of the house. The floor creaked beneath her feet as she neared the entrance of the master bedroom, and a shiver ran through her.

She made a quick right into the last of the smaller bedrooms. She'd save the best and biggest for last. That's what she told herself.

Gwen measured carefully, trying to avoid the grime on the base-boards and windowsills. When done, she moved toward the master bedroom with halting steps. Intellectually, she knew there was nothing in that space but an antique bed, dresser, bedside table, and lamp. Her body wouldn't cooperate with her mind, however. It insisted on sending out jolts of adrenaline whenever she got close.

Gwen inhaled and threw open the door. The view that greeted her was both startling and comforting. This was what she would sell. Not the home's invisible past, but this very visible panorama before her.

She tossed her pad and pen onto the bed, one of the few pieces of furniture that remained from Fiona's father's days. It was a lovely antique, and even Maricela agreed it would be perfect when staging the house for sale. It was a good thing Sondra had been found on the floor. If she'd been on the bed, it would've gone, no matter how perfect it was.

Good thing? Gwen shook her head. Poor choice of words. There was nothing good about Sondra's death.

The room was not only larger than the other bedrooms, but also contained a window seat and several nooks. Consequently, it took Gwen longer to get its dimensions. It would've been easier if she'd had someone to hold the other end of the tape, but she didn't want to bother Lance. She could hear the low murmur of the men's voices through the floor. He was busy.

As she stepped away from a window, she picked up her pencil from the sill where she'd set it and stared. The sill was clean. Completely dust free. It almost shone. Why would someone clean only one of the bedrooms?

She glanced at the other surfaces in the room. All clean. Dust free. It made no sense. Something else niggled at her.

The bed.

She'd noticed it when she'd entered, but it hadn't registered as unusual until now. She turned slowly and examined it. It was there. She hadn't imagined it. One of the pillows was indented, the case wrinkled as if someone's head had recently rested there. But whose?

1.2.5

GWEN STARED at the hollow space. Could Fiona have taken a nap in the master bedroom on one of her visits to the house? It didn't seem likely. She didn't even want to oversee the renovations. Fiona had such a negative reaction to the house; Gwen couldn't imagine her relaxing in the very room where Sondra's body was found.

She ran a hand over the pillow sham, erasing the indent, but her questions weren't erased as easily. Had it been Lance? He had the code to the lockbox. He could've dropped in over the weekend, gotten tired, and... And what? Laid down in an upstairs bedroom?

"Gwen?" His voice startled her out of her thoughts. She glanced up. He stood in the doorway looking at her with a quizzical expression. "You're deep in thought. I called you twice."

"Oh, sorry." She gave him an apologetic smile. "What's up?"

"I'm available if you want to talk."

As they trooped down the stairs, Gwen considered asking him about the clean windowsills and the imprint on the pillow. She couldn't figure out how to state the question without sounding accusatory, though. And, really, was there anything wrong with him taking a break on the only piece of furniture in the place?

"The plumber is going to send me an estimate," he said as they entered the kitchen. "The problems aren't as extensive as I thought, so that's good,"

She noticed he'd set up two camp chairs and a small folding table where the breakfast nook ought to be. The bed was no longer the only furniture in the house, then. She'd keep an eye on it. If she saw any other signs it was being used, she'd ask him about it. If she took the listing, of course.

They sat, and Lance outlined his plans. They were good plans. The house would take more work than she'd originally thought, but there would be less for buyers to dicker over when it was done.

He pulled out a color wheel next and showed her his top paint choices. He said he'd bring samples by the next day. Gwen realized that if she took the listing, it would keep her very busy. Between her other properties and the kids, she was already very busy. Which was an excellent argument for leaving it alone.

Then again, when it sold, she'd make more money than she'd ever made from one deal, and that was hard to walk away from. Honestly, she didn't understand why she was so conflicted.

"So." Lance leaned back in the chair. "Looks like we'll be seeing a lot of each other for a while."

Gwen examined his face. Was he flirting? Stating a fact? She couldn't read him. "I haven't sent Fiona an agreement yet."

He raised an eyebrow. "No? Why not?"

She hesitated. Maybe it would be a good thing to discuss this with an unbiased party. Lance didn't know her, didn't care about her. He hadn't sworn to love and protect her like Art. And, unlike Maricela, he'd never been attacked in a vacant house. Lance would give her a professional opinion based on the facts, not one clouded by emotion.

"There are some who think I shouldn't list the property," she said.

"Because of the murder?" His eyes widened in surprise.

"Yes."

"Forgive me for saying it, but that's not logical."

Gwen lowered her eyes. It was difficult to look into his clear green gaze while attempting to explain something so tangled. "They think—since the first agent was killed here—the house might be..." She searched for the right word.

"I can't believe it's dangerous if that's what they are worried about." He emphasized the word they as if he didn't believe they existed. "I did a little research over the weekend. The police think it was a random attack, like you said on Friday."

"What if they're wrong?"

"The police?"

"Yes."

Lance was quiet for a moment, and Gwen lifted her gaze to his face again. His brow was furrowed, and his cheek indented as if he was biting it. Finally, he said, "If there were a plane crash on Tuesday, would you cancel your flight on Wednesday?"

"No."

"Why?"

"Well, because there are hundreds, thousands, of flights every day. Only a minuscule number crash. But we're talking about the same plane."

Lance leaned his elbows onto his knees. "Right. The only valid reason to cancel a flight because of a prior crash is if the plane that went down was the same kind of aircraft as the one you have a ticket for."

"So, you think I shouldn't take this listing?"

He held up a finger. "And you knew that model had a history of problems."

She realized what he was saying. "But no one other than Sondra Olsen has been murdered in this house."

He raised his palms. "Exactly. No pattern. It was arbitrary."

Lance's arguments were logical, but Don Gordon's statement about opening Pandora's box popped into her mind. "That's not the only reason."

"Don't tell me you're worried about ghosts or auras or effluvia or something."

She snorted. "No. It's an association thing."

"You mean, you don't want to become known as the Realtor who handles murder scenes?"

"Something like that."

"Listen, if you sold this house, I'd figure you could sell anything." He shot her a lopsided smile. "I'd give you my listing in a heartbeat."

Gwen couldn't help but return the grin. "You're in the business. You understand."

"People who can afford to buy and sell multimillion dollar properties in Orange County are savvy, not superstitious. The gawkers from inland aren't your potential clients anyway."

He had a point. "You're right." She waved a hand. "About all of it. I don't know why I've been on the fence."

"Fences are uncomfortable. The posts..." He made a face. Gwen laughed.

"This house is going to sell for a bundle when it's done," he added.

"I'd be crazy not to take the listing," she said.

"Fiona seems like an easy person to work with."

"She's great." Gwen nodded in agreement.

He tapped his chest. "Everybody says I'm a good guy."

"I'm sure you are."

"Then what's the hold up?"

Gwen stood. "Right." She moved toward the dining room.

"Where are you going?"

"To the office." She grabbed her purse from the kitchen counter. "To write the contract."

1.2.6

THE OFFICE WAS quiet when Gwen arrived. Most of the agents were out previewing the homes that came on the market over the weekend, which was fine by her. She needed peace and quiet to write up the contract for Fiona. It was a standard form, but since she'd be monitoring the renovations, she needed to amend it.

Gwen made her way past the reception desk in the bright lobby and entered the shared workspace behind it. The agents used to have their own cubicles, but the agency had updated recently to an open office plan in trendy grays and blues. She dropped her purse on her desk, logged onto her computer, pulled up the contract form, and got to work.

As she was finishing up, she heard voices in the lobby. A minute later, Maricela, Carolyn and two more agents made their way into the room.

Maricela perched on the edge of Gwen's desk. "Where were you this morning?"

"Laguna." She said the word firmly, anticipating her friend's negative reaction.

"You decided to list it." It wasn't a question.

"There's no reason not to."

Maricela raised her eyebrows but didn't respond.

"No good reason," Gwen said. She considered telling her about the conversation she'd had with Lance that morning, but what was the use? Maricela's opinion on the topic was emotional. Logic wasn't going to sway her.

"It would be hard to pass up," Maricela said, surprising Gwen.

"I'm glad you understand."

Her friend reached out a hand and placed it on top of Gwen's. "I do." She closed her eyes for a second. When she opened them again, she focused on Gwen. "I need to get rid of my fears, but not by giving them to my friends."

Gwen felt her shoulders relax. It would be good to be able to share the ups and downs of this deal with her friend. That wasn't possible before this moment.

Maricela stood. "Want to get lunch later?"

"Can't," Gwen said. "Jason left his lunch at home. I told him I'd drop something off for him."

Maricela rolled her eyes. "Kids." She walked to the rear of the large room to her own desk.

Gwen checked her watch. She had just enough time to drop by Fiona's new studio, have her sign the contract, pick up a burger from In-and-Out, and get to the school by Jason's lunch break. First, she'd hit the bathroom.

She left the contract next to her purse and jacket and walked down the hall. The first thing she saw when she returned was Don Gordon. He stood at her desk, Fiona's contract in his hands. Irritation flushed through her, making her cheeks flame.

She marched toward him. "What are you doing?"

He glanced up and gave her an unperturbed smile. "So, you decided to list the Laguna house."

Gwen snatched the papers from his hands. "I did."

He leaned against her desk. "Hope you know what you're doing."

The irritation turned to anger. "I've been an agent for five years, Don. I'm pretty sure I know what I'm doing."

"Oh, I don't doubt your professionalism."

Gwen shouldered her purse and grabbed her jacket. "What a relief."

"This kind of publicity can impact a career and not for the better. That's all I'm saying."

"Thanks for your concern."

He held up both hands in surrender. "I care about you, Gwen. Don't want to see you step into something messy."

Because he wanted to step into the deal. He didn't say that, but Gwen was fairly certain he was one of the agents that had contacted Fiona about putting the house back on the market. "Again, thanks for your concern." She walked past him and strode toward the door, anger seething.

The drive to Dana Point took fifteen minutes. By the time she pulled into the parking lot behind Fiona's new Pilates studio, her blood had cooled. Don was a jerk, but he hadn't done any harm. Everybody had to deal with jerks from time to time. It was probably good for her character.

Gwen climbed an exterior stairway and pushed open a glass door at the top. The sounds of construction greeted her. She entered an empty room flanked by large windows. "Fiona?" She called over the din.

Nobody answered. She crossed the space and walked through a doorway into a brilliantly lit space. Sunlight beamed through a wall of windows on her left and reflected off a mirrored wall opposite. Her gaze was drawn to the view of the Dana Point Harbor and the sparkling ocean beyond. It was beautiful.

The shots of a nail gun nearby reminded her of her errand.

"Fiona?" she called again. A moment later, her client popped out of a doorway at the end of the wall of mirrors.

"Gwen, hi. Sorry I didn't hear you." She glided across the floor, placed a hand on Gwen's arm and pulled her toward the front room. "Sorry it's so noisy in here."

"Not a problem."

"How do you like my Fishbowl?" she asked when they reached the relative quiet of the foyer.

"Fishbowl?"

"That's what I'm thinking of calling the studio." Fiona gestured to the windows. "Because of the view."

"I like it," Gwen said. She wasn't much of a Pilates devotee. But if she ever decided she couldn't live without washboard abs, this would be the place she'd get them.

"What do you have for me?"

Gwen pulled the contract from her purse and handed it to Fiona. "It's pretty standard, just one or two things on the last page to cover the renovations."

Fiona skimmed the first pages, then read the final page more carefully. When she was done, she looked at Gwen. "Perfect. Where do I sign?"

"Keep that for your records. I'll send you a document online when I get back."

Fiona folded the papers. "Lance comes highly recommended." Her eyes returned to Gwen's face. "But he's a perfectionist, which is why I need you to help me keep the costs to a minimum."

"I'll do my best," Gwen said. "But if we want the place to sell... "

"I know—but look around you. I've put most of my inheritance—the cash, I mean—into this place. We're running over-budget."

"Contractors tend to underestimate things." A table saw revved in the other room as if adding an exclamation point to Gwen's statement.

"Time and money," Fiona said in a loud voice.

"When the house sells, you'll recoup the expenditures," Gwen shouted back.

Fiona held up a hand. Her fingers were crossed.

1.2.7

THE LINE for In-and-Out wrapped around the building. Gwen glanced at the car's clock and headed to a less popular fast-food restaurant. Jason wouldn't be happy, but teenage boys who forgot their lunches couldn't be choosy.

She found him sitting on the school steps. His brow furrowed when he saw the logo on the bag. "The line was too long," she said.

"Thanks," he accepted the bag, already dark with grease, without complaint, kissed her cheek, and ran off in the direction of the school quad.

Gwen's stomach rumbled. She didn't eat fast food, but the rich scents of meat and French fries reminded her she hadn't had anything but coffee yet. She entered the school.

There was a nice Tex-Mex place nearby. She'd kidnap Art and take him out on her business credit card. She'd just signed the biggest listing of her career. That deserved a celebration, didn't it? She might even get a margarita.

Gwen climbed the stairs in the echoey stairwell, dodging kids as they rushed past her and out the double doors into the sunshine. Their voices bounced off the tile walls. Their laughter boomeranged through the hallways. The building hummed with the energy of the students who filled it.

Art's job was both exhilarating and exhausting. She understood why he loved it despite the fact that he could make more elsewhere. Years ago, when Emily was a toddler and Gwen stayed at home with her, this had been a constant source of irritation.

Gwen had wanted Art to get a better job. Better, as in more money. He felt he'd already found his place in the world. Which was why the principal position was so exciting. It satisfied them both. The pay was significantly higher than his teacher salary had been, which made Gwen happy. And he got to stay at his beloved St. Barnabas, which made him happy.

A rope of tension tightened around her throat. If he lost the position because of Brian McKibben's accident, it would be a terrible blow. To both of them.

Gwen made a left on the second floor and walked down the corridor. She pushed open the door marked PRINCIPAL and entered. Millie, his assistant, wasn't at her desk, and the door to the inner office was shut.

She moved toward it but paused. Raised voices came to her through the heavy wooden door. A man's and a woman's.

The male voice belonged to Art. She'd recognize it anywhere, but she didn't know who the female was. It wasn't Millie. Of that, she was sure. Millie had a throaty alto, and after having served as assistant to the principals of St. Barnabas for the past twenty-five years, nothing ruffled her feathers. The woman in Art's office was definitely ruffled.

Gwen leaned closer to the door, but couldn't make out their words, only the tone of their voices. Art's was a low, comforting rumble. The woman's spiked and flattened and occasionally broke like ocean waves on a choppy day.

What should she do? Gwen walked to the hallway and back to the door again. If Millie had been there, she'd have rescued Art from the emotional situation inside.

Gwen lifted a hand to knock, to sub in for the missing Millie, but dropped it to her side again. Millie would know what was going on. She'd know why the woman was upset. Gwen was clueless.

She stood in indecision for a long moment, straining her ears, but it was no good. She couldn't tell what they were saying. Lunch would have to be a solo affair.

As she turned toward the hallway again, the door to the inner office flew open. Gwen caught her breath and backed toward the wall. A young, blond woman, attractive despite her red-rimmed eyes, hurried past.

Art filled the doorway, his face a mask of concern, his gaze glued to the woman's retreating form. It took a full minute before he acknowledged Gwen's presence. "Hi." It was all he said, no explanation, no surprise.

"What was that all about?"

He inhaled and exhaled slowly before answering. "That was Olivia Richards. Brian's mother."

"Oh." The noose of tension Gwen had felt earlier, tightened.

Art gave a quick shake of his head. "Actually, it's good news. The brain swelling is down. The doctors want to back off the sedatives."

"Then why all the drama?"

"She got a letter from the board." Art blew out a loud breath. "There won't be any scholarship money for Brian next school year."

"Why?" The word burst from Gwen. It seemed so unfair to punish the family, with all they were going through.

"I don't know for certain, but I believe they're playing politics, protecting themselves. I think they're trying to build a case against Brian, make him out to be a problem child."

The tightness in Gwen's throat eased just a little. "Is he? He was suspended."

"No." She jumped at the force of Art's voice. "He is not a problem child. He did, however, punch a board member's son."

Silence rang around them as Gwen tried to understand what Art was telling her. "Did you suspend him to..." She couldn't finish the sentence. It seemed so accusatory.

"Curry favor?" He turned, walked into his office, and sank into a chair. "I didn't think so at the time."

Gwen followed and sat in the chair next to him. "What do you mean, you didn't think so?"

"Exactly that. Brian punched another child, made his nose bleed.

That's a suspendable offense. It's not fair, but the scholarship kids are often held to a higher standard. I wanted to nip the thing in the bud, so he wouldn't lose his tuition money."

"And it just happened to be a board member's kid," Gwen said.

Art dropped his eyes to the floor. "That's what I told myself."

She wanted to reach out, to wrap an arm around his shoulders, but she found herself frozen in her seat. "And now?"

"And now, I don't know." He lifted his head and stared at her. "What if I was harder on him than I should've been, because I want this job so badly?"

"No." Gwen stood, the confusion that had kept her immobile suddenly evaporating. "No, that's not you." She marched to the far wall and back, using big hand gestures to emphasize her words. "You turned down that position at Sand Canyon Christian three years ago, even though they offered you almost twice what you were making here."

"I didn't like the curricula—"

She cut him off. "You never applied for the public school position I wanted you to apply for."

"I couldn't navigate the politics in the public school."

"Exactly," Gwen said. "You have scruples. It's something that has irked me about you for years."

He huffed a small laugh. "I appreciate your saying that."

"I'm saying it because it's the truth."

Neither spoke for several seconds, then they both spoke at once.

"Let's get out of here," Gwen said.

"I'm going to bat for Brian," Art said.

She sat next to him again. "Let's get lunch and talk about it."

"I don't think I can eat."

"Just get a coffee if you're not hungry, but you need to get out of here. Clear your head."

Art pulled Gwen toward him and rested his cheek on the top of her head. "I wouldn't be able to relax, but thank you."

"What are you going to do?"

"I'm going to call the director. Tell him what I think about pulling Brian's financing."

A jolt of nervousness coursed through Gwen. Whether she liked it or not, Art cared more about his principles than the family's financial health. A part of her admired him for that. Another part of her felt betrayed by it.

She pulled away from him. "Be careful how you word it."

He nodded but didn't say anything. They'd replayed similar scenes dozens of times over the course of their marriage.

Gwen walked down the stairs toward the big double doors more slowly than she'd climbed them. She'd never told Art about the contract Fiona had signed that morning. The deal now seemed even more fortuitous, although she felt less like celebrating.

Her appetite was gone, as well. Thinking about the phone call Art was about to make sent a flurry of wings flapping in her stomach. She crossed the parking lot, clicked open the Honda doors, and climbed inside. As she started the ignition, a thought struck her. If Art lost his job at St. Barnabas, he'd be forced to find something else. Maybe that wouldn't be such a terrible thing, after all.

1.2.8

WEDNESDAY AFTERNOON, Gwen stopped by The Leaky Barrel. The stupid bell with its heavy clapper startled her as it always did, regardless of how many times she'd been there. It reverberated through Gwen's skull. Really, if this place didn't have the best wine selection in South Orange County, she'd stop frequenting it.

Afternoon light from a picture window fell in beams on the bar, spotlighting the owner. He spoke into a phone but wiggled his fingers at her in acknowledgment. She walked over to a wall of red wines. Too often when she shopped here, Mo followed her from shelf to shelf, giving her more information than she wanted. He knew his wine, but it was a relief to wander without the education today.

What should she bring Maricela? A pinot? She dropped her purse on the floor and ran her finger over a row of pinot noirs.

Art had been so stressed lately, she wanted to plan something nice, something relaxing and romantic. Jason told her that morning that he had an overnight event with his youth group from church on Friday— Valentine's Day. Tyler had also been invited to a sleepover at a friend's house that night. With two of her three children away, she only had to find someplace for the third. Gwen called Julissa, Maricela's daughter.

Julissa was Emily's favorite babysitter. She was old enough to be responsible, but not old enough to be boy crazy. Generally, she came to Gwen and Art's house, but this Friday, Emily was spending the night at the Alvarez home. Julissa would take cash. Maricela wouldn't, but she never looked a gift bottle of wine in the mouth.

Gwen selected a pinot noir for Maricela, then turned down the aisle of red blends. She picked out two bottles of her favorite, a Meritage from a small vineyard on the Central Coast. It wasn't easy to find. The Leaky Barrel was the only place that carried it locally.

The name was appropriate considering the effect it had on Art the last time they'd shared a bottle. It was called Red Ravish. Things had been sluggish in the bedroom of late, but Valentine's Day seemed the perfect time to revive their love life.

Gwen brought her purchases to the front of the shop. "Anything else?" The owner smiled. His front teeth were too small for his incisors. It made his face look like Rocket's when the kids got too close to his rawhide bone.

"Just these." Gwen put her bottles on the counter.

"A lovely blend and it ages well. It's a particular favorite of mine," he said as he rang up the Ravish.

"Yes, it's very good."

"You know what they say, wine and women improve with age."

Gwen's lips tightened. That was a such a sexist statement. Did he know she was turning forty in a couple of weeks? Was he teasing her?

She examined his face, but he seemed focused on the cash register, not her.

"Cash or charge?" he asked.

Gwen reached for her purse. It wasn't there. A stab of panic came and quickly receded. She'd set her bag on the floor near the pinot noirs, and the shelf was directly behind her. She retrieved the purse, paid, and left the shop.

As she drove home, Mo's comment about women replayed in her mind. It stung, more than it should. "I am not my mother," she said aloud.

What happened to her mother wouldn't happen to her. She wouldn't allow it to. But the feeling of impending doom had been looming larger and larger as her birthday approached, regardless of what she told herself.

The night of her mother's fortieth, she'd cooked her own birthday dinner—chicken, baked potatoes, and broccoli au gratin. Gwen's father never took them out. He always said, why eat in a restaurant when the best chef in the county lived in his own house. The words made her mom smile, but Gwen secretly thought she'd have enjoyed a restaurant meal once in a while.

For dessert, her mother made her famous chocolate layer cake. Gwen bought a pack of candles on her way home from school, sneaked into the kitchen after finishing her dinner, and placed four on its top. Then she carried the flaming cake into the dining room, singing "Happy Birthday" at the top of her lungs. It was the last time Gwen could remember seeing her mom look truly happy.

She turned onto her street and something warm and cozy wrapped itself around her. When she got home, she'd have to put the miserable memories on pause and deal with the busyness of life—her crazy, comfortable life.

The relief quickly turned to concern when she pulled up to the house. Art's car wasn't in its spot. Wednesdays were his days to pick up the kids. He brought them home when school let out and worked in his home office until dinner.

"Hello," she called as she entered the house.

"Mommy." Emily slid around the corner in stockinged feet and skidded right into Gwen. Rocket was at her heels.

"Hi, peach." Gwen kissed the top of her head and scratched the dog. "Where's your dad?"

"He went out. Jason thinks he's watching us, but I don't need anybody to watch me."

"It's always good to have someone older around," Gwen said, distractedly.

She moved into the kitchen and stowed her wine in the back of the cupboard. She wanted Friday night to be a surprise. "Where's Jason?"

"He's in the backyard. He and Tyler are working on that go-cart." Emily said, then disappeared down the hallway toward her bedroom.

Gwen opened the backdoor and stepped into the yard. Her boys were bent over a piece of wood, two sets of old lawn mower wheels lying nearby. "Hi," she said. They each gave her a quick glance and a mumbled greeting.

"Where's Dad?"

Tyler pushed his blond bangs from his forehead. "He went somewhere."

"I figured that," Gwen said. "I'm trying to find out where."

Jason said, "Hold this," in an irritated voice.

"I'm trying," Tyler said.

She wasn't going to get any more from them, so she returned to the house. Obviously, if she wanted to know where Art was, she was going to have to ask him. The children were clueless. Her purse was on the counter where she'd left it. She fished around, found her phone at the bottom of the bag, and hit Art's number. The call rang six times and went to voice mail.

She stared at her phone screen and bit her lip. This wasn't like him. She opened her texts.

Where are you?

She watched the screen to see if the little bubble blinked to show he'd seen the message and was responding, but nothing happened.

Art didn't come home until dinner was eaten and the kids were on their way to bed. Gwen was seated on the couch, surfing channels, when she heard the front door open and close. A moment later, he entered the living room and sank into his brown chair. He looked pale and drawn.

Gwen turned off the television. "Where have you been?"

"At the hospital."

Her heart stumbled out an extra beat. "Brian?"

Art nodded.

"I thought he was doing better," she said.

"It's not life or death any longer." Art rubbed a hand over the stubble on his chin. "It's about quality of life."

"Quality?"

"There's some brain damage."

An ache formed in Gwen's chest. "Is it bad?"

"That's just it, they don't know. Won't know for a while. Olivia is beside herself."

"Olivia?"

"His mother," Art said.

Gwen knew who he was referring to, but when had she become just plain Olivia? When Art referred to her in the past, it was always Olivia Richards or Ms. Richards.

"I didn't feel I could leave her, not in that state."

So, Art was responsible for Olivia's emotional condition now? This was a new development, one she didn't like. "You could've called."

"Had to turn off my phone. Hospital rules."

"I didn't know where you were." Gwen sounded angry, even to her own ears. She cleared her throat.

Art glanced at her. "I told the kids where I was going."

Of course he had. Why he believed they'd relay the information was another topic for another day. Her irritation dissipated. "Did you eat?"

His mouth turned up in an imitation of a smile. "I had a sandwich in the hospital cafeteria. It was the only way I could get Olivia to eat anything."

Now he was responsible for Olivia's nutritional welfare as well as her emotional well-being. "There's spaghetti if you're still hungry." Gwen kept her voice even.

Art stood. "Thanks, but I think I'll head to bed. I'm done in."

He left without kissing her goodnight, and the room suddenly seemed empty and quiet. Gwen reached for the TV remote again. As she did, her phone pinged with a text message.

> Can you bring the paint tomorrow?

It was Lance. She'd told him she'd pick up an extra gallon and take it to the house this week.

Sure.

And the ceiling lights?

The question pinged almost immediately.

Yup.

A smiley emoji wearing sunglasses came back, and Gwen grinned at her phone screen. Lance was okay, not the stuck-up player she'd thought when they'd first met. She liked him.

MOLLY: We'll have to leave it here for now. I don't know about you, but I'm sensing a little sexual tension between Gwen and Lance. That kind of thing is always dangerous when hubby is distracted, which he definitely is.

You may be wondering what all this family drama has to do with REK, but stay with me, people. You'll totally find out. The relationships play a critical role as the story unfolds.

However, if you're anxious to get back to our killer, you'll be happy to know that next time we'll be hearing quite a bit from him. We'll hear what he's thinking and planning currently in the story timeline as well as some of his history. Let's just say, he didn't have a happy childhood.

If you haven't joined the conversation in the Facebook group, you're missing out. We've been having some great discussions there. In fact, the question of the week is: Do you think Gwen is overreacting to Art's concern for Brian and his mother? How would you feel if it were you?

Join me next time for more *Murders Under the Sun.*

(cue music)

VO: This episode is brought to you by Nightshade Gallery in Laguna Beach, for collectors of avant-garde fine art. *Murders Under the Sun* is edited by Jim Wilbourne, theme music is by Eclectic Blends, and I'm your host, Molly Shure.

part four

MURDERS UNDER THE SUN
 SEASON ONE; EPISODE THREE

MOLLY: Welcome back to *Murders Under the Sun*. I'm Molly Shure, your host.

Okay, people, things get seriously strange in this episode. We'll hear from the Real Estate Killer not once but twice, and these entries give us insight into a truly warped mind.

Before we dive in, I want to acknowledge your comments on the page this week. They were all over the board. Some thought Gwen was being completely paranoid, some thought she should be concerned. As a number of you pointed out, the opinions were deeply personal, most likely related to the posters' life experiences.

And speaking of life experiences, I got an interesting question from a listener this week, I thought I'd read her email then answer it on the air. I've received similar questions in the past few weeks.

Tricia McKinney wrote:

Hi Molly, love the show.

My question isn't about Gwen or what's happening in The Cliff House, *though. It's about you.*

I know you told us you were a journalist and these crimes piqued your interest because you thought you saw a connection between them, but what drew you to crime reporting to begin with? I've always wondered why cops or journalists willingly spend so much time on such hard topics.

Again, love the show.

> *Best,*
> *Tricia*

Thanks for writing, Tricia. My curiosity—maybe that's the wrong word. My obsession—that's a better word. My obsession with crime started when I was in college. My original major was English. I planned to be a teacher, but in my second year something happened that altered everything.

I had a roommate, a bestie kind of roommate, not the kind you put up with. Melissa Shilling. She was smart, pretty, funny, and just a great friend. Anyway, right after winter break, Mel went out to party on a Saturday night and never came back.

The police investigated for months, but the trail stopped at The Raven's Perch, a bar we used to go to all the time. They never found her. That event changed my life, and it changed the trajectory of my career.

If my crime reporting can raise red flags, ring a warning bell, and help even one woman avoid Mel's fate, I've done something good with my life.

Now that you know a little more about me, let's get back to our regularly scheduled show. I wanted to point out something you may have already noticed. I haven't revealed REK's identity. In fact, I've had to hide some of your comments on the Facebook page. No offense, guys, but I don't want spoilers.

I know some of you followed the case in the news, and you already know who he is. However, there are those out there who don't. I'd like to keep it a surprise for them.

The story will have more impact if we travel

this road the way Gwen travelled it—feel her fears and doubts and suspicions, go through the mental processes she goes through. Is she being sabotaged? And if she is, who's the culprit? These were the questions constantly running through her mind. Let them run through yours. Keep listening, and you'll learn REK's identity when Gwen does.

Okay, enough of that. Here's the first excerpt from REK's memoir manuscript.

1.3.2

AFTER DOING SOME RESEARCH, I discovered the easiest thing would be to bug Gwen Bishop's cell phone. She was the listing agent on the beach house, therefore she would be the first to know about open houses or potential buyers.

According to the internet, it was a relatively simple process. You only needed to install a spy app onto the phone of the person you wanted to keep tabs on. The tech wasn't complicated. Gaining access to the phone proved trickier.

Thankfully, Gwen keeps her phone in her purse and tends to leave her purse lying around. I had to work quickly when opportunity knocked, but it was a brief process. Just upload the app to her phone, then connect my account. I can now monitor her texts and calls directly from my phone or computer.

They aren't very interesting. Most revolve around things needed by her children, or things she needs from her husband. So I decided to do a test to be sure this was the phone she used for work. Since I bugged her phone, I thought it only appropriate to bug the Cliff Drive house as well. Not the way I'd originally intended, however.

I entered through the basement window, the one covered by siding and hidden behind a rose bush. I don't think anyone's aware of it, at least not yet. And I brought a box full of little friends with me. You can get anything on the internet.

It was difficult for me to sully my home, but the end justifies the means. I set up my roach motel in the living room, made sure it would achieve its purpose, and turned to go. I wanted to stay, but I couldn't. Renovations were underway. Workmen would be coming and going.

I crossed the foyer toward the basement stairs, and a memory kicked me in the chest with the force of a panicked horse. I saw my eighteen-year-old self, knocking on that very front door. It was the only time I'd met my father. I'd successfully blocked the event from my mind until now.

My mother knew beyond a shadow of a doubt who'd impregnated her. When I was conceived, he was keeping her in a very nice little cottage and paying all the bills, so she had no need for other friends. It wasn't until he learned of the pregnancy that he abandoned her.

Oh, he paid dearly for her silence. Gave her the cottage and a healthy sum of money to keep her in groceries until she got her figure back. But I never saw a dime of it.

I wanted to go to college. I'd had good grades in high school. Not good enough to get a scholarship, but good. I knew my father was quite wealthy. Since he hadn't contributed to my needs up to this point, I figured he owed me something. A college education seemed like the least he could do.

When I rang the bell, this very bell, my father answered the door himself. In my mind's eye, his ghost now strode purposefully across the foyer and yanked open the door, a look of annoyance on the handsome face.

He'd had no idea who I was. He just stood there in his shirt-sleeves, glaring at me, and asked, "Can I help you?"

"Yes, you can," I said.

He cocked his head to the side and waited. Clearly, he didn't plan to ask me in. He must not have noticed the family resemblance that was so apparent to me. I remember that I hadn't wanted to break it to him on his doorstep. I thought he ought to be sitting down, but he gave me no choice.

"Hello, Father," I said.

I'm not sure what I was expecting. As I said, I'd blocked out the memory until this very moment. I know I'd fantasized about him throwing his arms around me and welcoming me into the family with tears in his eyes. But that was a Dickens novel, not reality. More probably, he'd want to maintain the secret of my birth.

I could understand that. Respect it even. He had a wife and a daughter. I would be hard to explain. But maybe he'd want to meet his only son for a drink now and again.

His expression changed in an instant. His eyes narrowed. His face grew stony. "Excuse me?"

"Hello, Father," I said again.

"Who are you?"

"Your son." That seemed obvious, based on how I'd addressed him. And I shouldn't be a complete surprise. He'd known about my birth.

"I don't have a son." His voice was as cold as his visage.

"And yet, here I am. Can't we discuss this inside?" I'd said the words as lightly as I could.

He stared at me for a long moment. So long I thought he was considering letting me in, but then he said, "If you think you're going to get money from me by perpetrating a fraud, you're sadly mistaken."

The door began to close. I stuck my foot in the opening. "This is no fraud, Father.

"Get your foot out of my doorway," he said. I could smell his anger.

"Please... "

His voice grew low and menacing. "Get off my property, or I will call the police."

At that moment, I never wanted anything as much as I wanted to be let into this elegant house. As hopeless as the idea was, I'd longed to walk through this hall that opened into the sunlit rooms beyond, to chat over a drink, to dine with the family.

"Can't we talk about this?" The words struggled past my tightening throat.

"I'm asking you one more time to remove your foot from my doorway."

There was no point in getting into a wrestling match. I left.

The memory had taken so much out of me, I collapsed on the

bottom tread of the stairs leading up to the bedrooms. "It's my house now, Father," I said aloud. The words echoed through the empty foyer. They weren't entirely true, but they would be.

Another memory galloped back. That night, after I'd tried to plead my case, I walked down the public stairs to the beach. The tide was high. I sat on the bottom step of another stairway and removed my shoes and rolled up my pant legs. I waded into the whispering waves down the beach until I stood under the house.

It blazed with light from the French doors and windows that faced the ocean. I could see people moving around inside. A brown-haired woman walked back and forth between rooms. My father, head bent over a book, looked up every so often and laughed at someone I couldn't see. Rage had filled me. I belonged in that room. It was my birthright.

I'm not sure how long I stayed that first night, but at some point, I felt the water climb to the middle of my calves, sopping my pants. I needed to leave if I didn't want to go for a swim. As I turned away, movement in the window caught my eye.

It was a girl.

A lovely, red-haired girl. She stepped to the French doors to look out at the night. In the gleam of the lamplight, her hair glowed like a fiery halo.

Years later, I read in the paper that my father had donated a large sum of money, much more than a bachelor's degree would have cost, to the college I had hoped to attend. They put his name on a plaque in the wing of the building he helped to fund. His daughter, my half-sister, received a master's degree from the same school.

The vision faded, and I pulled myself to a standing position using the banister. That girl had gotten enough of his money. The house and its treasure would be mine. I moved toward the cellar steps. At the very least, it wouldn't be hers.

MOLLY: And there's the motive. Yes, yes, we already knew about the elusive treasure, but why all the subterfuge? Why not make an offer on the place? Why not introduce himself to Fiona? Chances are she'd be more welcoming than REK's father was.

But our killer was angry, rejected, bitter, and probably pretty insecure in his very narcissistic way. Actually, I did a little research on narcissists. According to some new studies, narcissistic personality disorder is often a reaction to extreme insecurity. More on that in the next episode.

Whatever his actual diagnosis, REK isn't thinking logically. He doesn't tackle life the way you or I would. If you don't agree with me, just wait until the end of this episode.

Now, let's hear from Gwen.

1.3.3

THE NEXT MORNING, Gwen picked up the paint on her way to Laguna Beach. The ceiling lamps were already in her trunk. She'd bought them on Tuesday with Fiona's approval.

Lance's truck wasn't on the street when she parked. Good, she'd been hoping to beat him. Fiona had asked for a report on the renovations. It would be easier to take notes without him looking over her shoulder.

Over the past week, she'd developed a whole new appreciation for the man. He wasn't just a pretty boy after all. He and his team had gotten a lot done in a short time. With hammer in hand, he was like one of those Nordic gods. She decided there ought to be a hurricane named after him.

He'd removed the rotted kitchen flooring and located another source of the mold smell in the attic. It was the result of a leaky section of roof. He had one of his men patch in new tiles, then he moved on to the bathrooms, just in case they were contributing to the home's pervasive perfume.

He had the plumber replace two toilets, four faucets and a shower head. Then gave each room a coat of fresh paint himself. Even the towel racks and electric switch plates gleamed.

The old musty odor had been replaced by the clean, sharp smells of new paint, wood polish, and cleaning products. The painters were coming in next week to do the downstairs and the bedrooms, but he wanted to paint the ceiling of the upstairs hallway and put up new overhead lighting before the weekend.

If someone told her last week she'd be coming here in the early hours of the day, alone, with only a slight jogging of her pulse, she wouldn't have believed them. The renovations had affected more than the house, however. Gwen's uneasiness became less and less with each improvement that was made.

She hefted a gallon of Soft Cotton flat enamel across the foyer and into the living room. The ocean reflected the newly risen sun. Flecks of gold and silver glimmered on its surface. If this were her home, she'd decorate to complement the daily show outside. She imagined herself with a cup of steaming coffee, lounging on a deep maroon couch settled across from both the brick fireplace and the wall of windows.

She wouldn't put up curtains or shades. She'd welcome the sky and ocean into the space. Privacy wasn't an issue. No one could see in. Not unless they stood on the sand and peered up, and who would do that?

Lost in thought, it was a minute or two before Gwen noticed the scurrying near her feet. Blinded by the light from the windows, at first she couldn't discern what the black specks scuttling across the hardwood were. When her eyes adjusted, she screamed.

The room was alive.

A brown river of cockroaches streamed from the fireplace. It parted before her and joined together behind. A few of the insects took a detour over the top of her sneakers. Huge water bugs crawled over their smaller cousins like military tanks crushing an enemy army.

Gwen dropped the can of paint and ran from the room into the front hall. Her gaze went almost involuntarily to the cellar door. She'd half expected to see it wide open, an army of roaches marching through the doorway into the house. That damp, dark place was a perfect breeding ground for crawling things.

A shudder wracked her body, and she bolted for the front door, slamming it behind her. She stood on the front porch and hugged herself until the shudders subsided. Then she turned toward the street.

Before she reached the gate, an awful thought hit her. What if she'd carried some of the revolting bugs outside with her. What if she took them home? She'd read about people carting home garage sale items that were infested and ending up with a houseful of the revolting things.

She kicked and stomped and pulled her bra away from her body in case one had fallen into her cleavage. Then she gave her purse three hard shakes. As she shook the bag, she heard the clank of keys. She'd forgotten to lock the door.

Before sticking her hand inside to rummage for the house key, she set the purse on the ground and kicked it. Nothing crawled out, but disgust made her fingers thick and clumsy. It took forever to fish out the set of house keys.

She returned to the front door with reluctant steps but couldn't seem to find the key that fit into the lock. The longer she stood by the door, the sweatier her hands became. On the third try, the keys slipped from her hand and clattered onto the stone stoop. She reached down to retrieve them and saw two brown insects crawling up the leg of her jeans.

Gwen yelped. She slapped them to the ground and trampled them in a crazy jig. Would this never end?

She scooped up the keys. This was it. She would lock up the damn house, go home, and take a long, long shower.

Breathing hard, she turned to the door again. Two more attempts, and she heard the bolt slide into place. Finally. She hurried to the street, a mantra revolving through her brain. Go home. Get clean. She had a sudden compassion for people with obsessive-compulsive disorder.

As Gwen walked around her car to the driver's side, her gaze fell on the two boxes of ceiling lights she'd promised to deliver. She stared at them stupidly for several seconds. Go home. Get clean. The words ganged up on another thought vying for her attention: Lance needs those.

It was another full minute before Gwen could convince her feet to walk toward the house again. Roaches were disgusting, yes, but they weren't dangerous. The pep-talk didn't stop the shudders that accompanied the brown river flowing through her brain.

Some people hated snakes, some hated spiders. Gwen had a pathological aversion to roaches. Funny, she'd recently had a conversation about this at the Friday night office get-together at the Barrel, and now here she was, facing an apocalypse of the damn things.

She carried the lights through the gate, set them on the porch, and fit the key into the lock again. Her hands were sticky with dried sweat, but she did it. The bolt clunked back. She knelt. With one hand, she pushed the door open a crack. With the other, she slid the boxes through.

The last thing she saw before slamming the door shut again, was a water bug about a foot from her nose, antennae waving. She raced toward the street, through the open gate, and almost ran into Lance.

"Whoa, what's the hurry?"

"Roaches." She only managed one word.

"As in small, brown bugs?"

She closed her eyes and nodded. "They're everywhere."

He furrowed his brow. "Really?"

"It's horrible."

"Want to show me?"

Gwen's eyes widened. "No."

Again, Lance's eyebrows moved toward each other.

"You can't miss them, trust me," she said. "They're all over the living room

"Not the kitchen? Or bathrooms?"

She ran a hand through her hair, then realized she was unconsciously checking for bugs and dropped it to her side. "I don't know. I never made it into the kitchen or the bathrooms."

"They usually come through the pipes. Maybe all the plumbing work drew them out of hiding?"

Gwen moved toward her car. She didn't want to think about the bugs anymore. "Don't know." She opened the car door and slipped inside.

"Hey." Lance bent to look through the passenger window. She rolled it down. "Did you remember the paint and the lights?"

"They're in the house."

"Good." He gazed at her through puzzled eyes. "You okay?"

She was acting weird. Her disgust for the roaches could be misconstrued for dislike of him, or anger, or who-knows-what. "I hate cockroaches."

"I'm not overly fond of them, either," he said.

"No." She gazed out her windshield, wishing she were looking at the freeway instead of the street the house was on. "I really hate them. It's like a phobia."

"Oh." He nodded slowly, understanding dawning. "Thought it was me."

Gwen gave him a small smile. "No, unless there's something I don't know about you."

"Like I keep them for pets?"

"Or you're really a cockroach alien like the one in *Men in Black*."

His eyes opened in mock horror. "Scary idea."

Lance was a contractor, not the owner of the home or even Fiona's agent. It wasn't fair to leave him to deal with the infestation, but Gwen couldn't make herself go back inside.

"Listen," she said. "Why don't you take the day off, and I'll see if I can get an exterminator in today."

"I was going to work on the second story. You said they're all in the living room."

"They might be upstairs." Gwen cringed at the thought. "I didn't go up."

"Still, they're small." He shrugged. "They don't bite. I can work around them."

The idea was horrifying. "No. Don't. I'll get someone in to take care of them."

Lance gazed at her through intense green eyes for several seconds before he finally said, "I'll take care of it."

"You don't ne—"

He cut her off. "Please, let me."

It would be wonderful to turn this over to him, to never have to think about those bugs again. "If you're sure."

He patted her car. "I'm sure. I'll get them all cleaned up before you ever set foot in that house again."

"Thank you." She watched him pull a toolbox from the bed of his truck and push through the creaky gate. He knew what he was walking into, and he was going anyway. That took courage. Her admiration for him went up a notch.

1.3.4

AFTER A LONG, hot shower, Gwen headed into the office. The Laguna house wasn't her only listing. It seemed a good day to focus on the others. If for no other reason than to take her mind off the bugs.

She threw herself into work, and by afternoon, she'd almost forgotten the crawly things. She was about to log off the computer for the day when her phone rang. It wasn't a number she recognized, but she picked up. "Gwen Bishop."

"Gwen, this is Christina Purcell from Tangent Realty in Newport. I heard through the grapevine that you've listed a property on Cliff Drive in Laguna."

Where had she heard that? "It's not actually on the market yet. It's being renovated."

"Even better. I have a very motivated buyer." Christina's voice purred. "I think they'll be willing to make an offer on the property in its current condition. The wife is a designer. She's looking for a challenge."

Gwen paused before responding. This is what Fiona wanted. She was worried about the cash outlay and would be happy to sell the property as is. So why was Gwen hesitating? "I'd have to discuss it with the owner," she finally said.

"Before you do that, and before I talk to my buyers, would it be possible for me to tour the house?"

A cockroach crawled across the screen of Gwen's mind. "It's kind of a mess."

"I realize that, but my buyers are out of state. They want me to send pictures, layouts, make recommendations, all that, before they fly in," Christina said.

"Well." Fiona wanted to be rid of that house. Why was Gwen dragging her feet?

"I'd really appreciate it." Christina sounded eager.

"There is something I need to disclose." Again, Gwen was hedging. Was it just the cockroaches?

"If you mean the murder, I already know. My buyers don't care." Christina laughed. "In fact, I think they're hoping it'll mean a discount."

"I don't know—"

Christina interrupted her, "I was kidding. But, seriously, I'll be in Dana Point tomorrow morning. I could swing by the house on my way back to Newport—around ten?"

If the roaches were still there, Gwen could cancel. "Alright. I'll meet you at the property at ten."

After they hung up, Gwen chewed her bottom lip and stared at the wall. This was good news, so why didn't it feel like it? She punched Lance's number into her phone. He answered after three rings.

"How's the roach problem?" she said after greeting him.

"The bug guy just left. They're gone."

"I thought it took lots of exterminator visits to get rid of roaches," Gwen said

"That's the weird thing. It wasn't an infestation."

"What do you mean? There were a thousand of them. I've never seen so many."

"They were in the fireplace, not the pipes like I thought," Lance said. "The trail came from a glob of sticky stuff in the chimney."

Gwen was confused. "The exterminator thinks they climbed onto the roof and fell down the chimney?"

"Maybe."

"But where did they come from in the first place?"

"This is the beach."

"What does that mean?"

"It means, roaches like damp places. They like the beach."

"You sure they didn't come from the cellar?"

"I don't think so. Why?"

"It's damp and dark." She didn't add and creepy, but the word popped into her mind in a cartoon bubble.

"We could have him spray down there. It needs to be cleared out anyway." He paused. "Should we get on that?"

"I'll ask Fiona," she said, but she wouldn't. Not yet. One thing at a time. She was still recovering from the roaches.

"Anyway," Lance said. "The good news is the bug guy is pretty sure he got them all. He doesn't think they had time to make nests or lay eggs."

"An agent called me today." Gwen changed the subject. She'd reached her threshold for discussions about cockroaches.

"Yeah?"

"She wants to tour the house tomorrow morning."

"There's a lot left to do." He didn't sound any more excited about showing the place than she was, but that was logical. Lance was the contractor. He made his money before the house sold. Her reaction was illogical.

"I know, but her clients aren't opposed to a fixer upper."

Lance grunted but didn't speak. Gwen could tell by the grunt he wasn't happy. "I'm not going to say anything to Fiona yet."

"Good." He sounded a little happier.

Maricela, Don, and Carolyn entered the office together. Don and Carolyn continued to their workstations, but Maricela stopped at Gwen's desk. Gwen pointed at her phone, held up one finger, then continued her conversation with Lance. "It may be nothing. Agents can be nosey about other agents' listings."

"Right." His tone was almost optimistic.

"What agent?" Maricela mouthed the words.

"Tell you later," Gwen mouthed back, then spoke into the phone again. "I just want to be sure the bugs are gone before I show the house." Maricela's eyes grew wide when Gwen mentioned bugs.

"They're gone," Lance said.

"What bugs?" Maricela said as soon as Gwen hung up. Gwen inhaled and filled her in on the cockroaches and what Lance had told her about the sticky substance in the chimney.

"His name is Lance?" She asked when Gwen was finished. It seemed a funny question in light of the horror she'd just shared.

"Yeah, Lance Fairchild."

Maricela's face clouded. "I know him."

"Oh?" Gwen could tell by her friend's expression; she knew him and didn't approve.

"He worked on the Levitt's house—my listing in Capo Beach."

"Did he do a good job?"

Maricela nodded, but her lips had tightened into a thin line.

"Why are you making that face, then?"

"What face?"

"Like you just ate a raw plantain."

Maricela shrugged. "I don't like him."

Gwen had a sudden urge to defend Lance but repressed it.

Maybe Maricela knew something she didn't. "Why?"

"He's a player."

"A player? You know this how?"

"I saw him in action. He was very friendly with Sarah Levitt."

"He was working for her. Probably wanted to be in her good graces."

"Wasn't as nice to her husband." Maricela hiked her purse strap higher on her shoulder and headed to her own desk. "Just be careful, chica. He's too handsome for his own good." That was delivered over her shoulder.

As Gwen watched her walk away, her gaze fell on Don Gordon. The man was studying Gwen, but when their eyes met, he dropped his to the papers on his desk. Open office plans might be attractive and popular, but sometimes she missed her private cubicle.

Art was in good spirits when Gwen got home. It seemed that Brian McKibben had woken up, moved his limbs, and spoken. "Olivia is so relieved," he said, wiping a drop of chicken soup from his chin.

The family sat at the kitchen table and ate dinner together on weeknights. It was old-school, but Art insisted on it. Gwen had learned to appreciate the tradition although it wasn't one she grew up with.

"She actually went home. She's going to sleep in her own bed instead of the chair in his hospital room," Art said.

"Oh?" Gwen wasn't sure how to respond. She was happy about the boy's recovery and, of course, sympathetic to the mother, but Art's enthusiasm was annoying.

"There is brain damage." Art's voice grew somber. "However, the doctors are optimistic."

"Will he be, like, stupid now?" Emily asked.

"No, squid-face," Tyler said. "Brain damage doesn't mean you're stupid. It means you can't do stuff like talk or walk."

"Don't call your sister names," Gwen said. Her childhood had been filled with episodes of bullying she was still recuperating from. Kids had a nose for the underprivileged, the different, those without a champion to defend them. Her children would not be bullies.

"We don't call people stupid," Art said, then turned his gaze on Tyler. "Brian may have some cognitive problems, but the brain is very elastic."

Gwen gazed at Art. How could the thing that had most attracted her to him have become the most annoying? He defended the weak. She loved that, but she was no longer in that category.

Jason was gazing out the window, lost in his own thoughts, but Tyler and Emily furrowed their brows at their father's comment.

"Not elastic like rubber bands." Gwen knew what they were thinking. "What Dad means is that the brain can repair itself."

"Oh," Tyler said.

"Then he'll get all better," Emily said.

"Right," Gwen said.

"Well, we're not out of the woods yet," Art said.

We? So, Art was now a 'we' with Olivia Richards?

"But things are looking up." He rubbed the top of Emily's head with his knuckles, then grinned at Gwen. "What do you say we go out for frozen yogurt?"

She'd been planning on having some quiet time with him after dinner to tell him about the cockroaches and the Newport agent, but Emily, Tyler, and even Jason were already moving toward the door. Her news would have to wait.

1.3.5

MOLLY: Reminds me of some of the conversations we had around the table when I was growing up. Although, I don't think I ever called my sister squid-face.

Anyway, the cockroaches gave me the shudders. I had a hard time reporting that segment. But it gets worse. Listen to what REK did next.

Here's another chapter from his memoir.

A group of rats is called a mischief. I thought the name was appropriate to the situation, but it isn't why I chose a rat for my next prank. The reason was much more practical.

One of my neighbors had a rat problem due to an apricot tree. He purchased half a dozen rat motels and filled them with poison. The oddly shaped black boxes were everywhere on my street, and the rats were dying like flies.

On two separate occasions this past month, I found rigid rats right on the front walkway. Thinking they might come in handy, I'd popped them in the freezer. In plastic bags, of course.

I pulled one out as soon as I heard Christina Purcell's call come through on Gwen's phone. Thankfully, the weather was warm, and the vermin defrosted quickly. So quickly, I put it in a shoe box and removed it to the car. My home was beginning to smell gamey.

Before heading to the Laguna house with my gift, I decided to follow Gwen home. I wanted to be sure she wasn't planning a surprise visit to the house. How awkward would that be?

That was the excuse I gave myself for trailing her around, but honestly, I had another motivation. With all my eavesdropping, I was beginning to feel I knew her and thought I sensed a kindred spirit. Gwen was as different from Sondra as a merlot from a Syrah. Just as mercenary—all those agents seem to be cut from the same greedy cloth. But Gwen is tougher. I would need the assistance of a real estate agent at some point. Having her in my corner could be an asset.

She pulled into her driveway in her sensible blue Honda and turned off the engine. She exited the car, but before she made it to the front door, a little blond-haired girl burst into the yard, raced across the grass, and threw her arms around her. It was sweet. Maybe a little too sweet.

Gwen laughed and hoisted the child off the ground. The girl wrapped her legs and arms around her mother and the two marched into the house looking more arachnid than human.

A pang started in my chest and ran down my arms. I closed my eyes and fisted my hands against the feeling. This had been happening all too frequently lately. The doctor said it wasn't physical, but something akin to a panic attack. What did he know?

My father died of heart failure. That's what the paper had said. What if bad hearts ran in the family? I would have no way of knowing that since I'd been denied access. That train of thought increased the pain, however, so I pushed it away and focused on my plans for the evening.

A workman had been replacing roof tiles at the house. I'd seen his ladder leaning against the side of the building. I could use it to get onto the roof but needed to wait until after dark. So I sat and watched Gwen and her family move from room to room in their mid-sized suburban home.

At dinner time, they sat at the kitchen table to eat. Together. Like a family in a TV sitcom. I wasn't sold.

I don't believe Gwen is the happy wife and mother she appears to be. There is a steel rod beneath all that soft skin and flowing hair. I'd been listening in on her business calls for a week. She's a fierce negotiator. If she wants something, watch out.

When the kitchen light flicked off and the bedroom lights flicked on, I started my engine. There was nothing more to see. I drove to Laguna in a melancholy mood. My task seemed less humorous and more ridiculous with every mile.

I would complete it. I'd plant the vermin. But I no longer believed it would accomplish anything. Gwen wouldn't be warned off by a dead rat any more than she'd been scared away by the roaches. I'm afraid it was going to take more than mischief, much more.

MOLLY: I told you he was warped. Now let's hear what happens when Gwen finds his surprise.

1.3.6

THE EVENING CAME AND WENT, and Gwen never had an opportunity to fill Art in on her day. When morning came, she decided that might not be a bad thing. It would be more fun to tell him she had an offer than that there'd been interest in the house. And if Christina Purcell never brought an offer, well, then she wouldn't have to share the bad news.

She got to Laguna at 9:45. She'd wanted to arrive earlier, check on the house, and make sure the place was as neat as it could be under the circumstances. But by the time she'd made school lunches, answered a call from another of her sellers, and combed the tangles from Emily's hair, she'd been lucky to get here when she had.

She exited the car, took in a deep breath of salt air and tried to center herself. An onshore breeze tossed clouds about in a cerulean sky. The ocean, smooth as glass, reflected the heavenly blue. It was a perfect day to showcase a beachfront listing.

Lance pulled up as she was clicking her locks shut. She waited for him to park. "Good morning." She was glad he'd arrived before she'd entered the house. She could use the moral support.

"Morning." He returned her smile. "What time is your agent getting here?"

Gwen headed toward the house. "She'll be here at ten."

She pushed open the gate, stepped through, and tottered a bit as her wedge-heeled sandals hit the uneven walkway.

"You okay?" Lance put a stabilizing hand on her back.

Stabilizing. That's what he'd become—a stabilizing force in her life.

Gwen understood Maricela's concerns. It was hard not to be attracted to Lance. To say he was handsome was an understatement, but his looks weren't his most dangerous attribute. At least, not as far as Gwen was concerned. It was his dependability and his thoughtfulness that made him perilous. She hadn't known he possessed those traits, so she hadn't hardened herself against them.

"I'm fine." Gwen hurried forward, away from the intimacy of his hand.

"Let me get the door." He walked around her.

Gwen allowed him to enter first. She trusted him when he said the bugs were gone, but the last time she'd been in the house... Her skin crawled at the memory.

When she stepped across the threshold, the entryway walls drove all thoughts of roaches from her mind. "Oh." She inhaled sharply. "It's beautiful. I love the color. Just a touch of yellow to warm—" Gwen, eyes on the freshly painted stairwell, walked straight into Lance's back.

He'd stopped abruptly. "What is that?" He smacked a hand over his nose and mouth.

The smell hit Gwen a nanosecond after his words.

Ripe. Sweet. Sickening. A wave of nausea broke over her, leaving moisture on her hairline and upper lip.

"Stay here," Lance said.

Gwen didn't. Instead, she backed out the front door and stood under the arms of the fig tree. She took deep, cleansing breaths of ocean air trying to flush away the stench.

It was at least ten minutes before Lance walked outside again.

"What is it?" Gwen asked.

"Something is dead." His lips curled in disgust. "Don't worry. It's not another real estate agent. Not unless it's a really small one. It's coming from the stove vent. A bird must have flown down, gotten stuck, and died. It happens."

"I thought there were caps or traps or something at the top of the vents," Gwen said.

"The cap was missing. I climbed out an upstairs window and checked the roof."

"Doesn't that seem a bit strange to you? Coincidental?" Gwen had a lot of time to think while she'd been waiting for him to return. "I mean, first the cockroaches, then, the day we're planning to show the place, a dead bird in the stove pipe?"

"Old places are unpredictable."

"But I've never heard of a sudden infestation of roaches coming from a chimney flue. And what was the sticky stuff that attracted them?"

"Figs?" He waved at the tree. "I'm just guessing, but it seems likely."

Gwen gazed up at the heavy branches. Most spread over the fence toward the street, but some did overhang the roof. Their spidery fingers reached toward the house as if trying to creep inside of it. Figs did seem the likely culprit. "We need to get rid of this tree."

"Agreed."

Another thought struck Gwen. "But the smell. You were here yesterday, right?"

"Yeah."

"Did you smell anything then?"

Lance shook his head.

"Wouldn't it have to build up? Wouldn't the smell get stronger the longer the... *thing*... the animal has been dead? If it's this overpowering today, you'd think you'd have smelled something yesterday. Even if it was faint."

"I don't know." Lance ran a hand through his hair. "The painters were here. Paint has a pretty strong odor. Maybe it masked it. Or maybe it's been there for a couple of days and just started to stink."

Neither said anything for a beat, then both spoke at once. "We better call—"

"You'll have to cancel—"

Gwen stopped talking.

"You'll have to reschedule your agent," Lance said.

"How do we get the bird out of the vent?"

"I don't know. I'll figure it out."

Gwen had almost forgotten Christina Purcell was on her way. A vision of Don Gordon staring at her from across the office entered her mind.

"Lance..." Gwen's voice faltered. "What if someone is sabotaging us?"

"Sabotaging?"

"Yes. I know it sounds silly, but there is a lot of money wrapped up in this house."

His face creased. "Who would do that?"

Gwen lifted a shoulder. "Maybe another agent who wants the listing."

"How would they get access?" He waved a hand toward the front door. "Unless you're giving out the lockbox code."

He was right. "No, I haven't given it to anyone."

The tense lines of his face melted into something softer. "Let's not get paranoid."

Gwen flushed. She shouldn't have confessed her fears about the home's history to him. He thought she was overreacting. Maybe she was.

"It's a strange coincidence, granted." He took her hand and squeezed it as if he'd read her thoughts. "But I think it's our phantom fig."

"The bird?"

"Sure." He gazed at the roof line. "There's decaying fruit all over the roof, attracting all kinds of critters."

"Hello." A bright voice interrupted their conversation. Gwen pulled her hand from Lance's grasp just as a blond head poked through the gate. "Gwen?"

"You must be Christina." Gwen moved toward her; the hand Lance had held now outstretched.

They shook, and Christina glanced around Gwen toward the house.

"I'm so sorry," Gwen said.

Christina cocked her head to one side, smile still plastered in place.

"Something has fallen down the stove vent and died." Gwen made a face. "The smell inside is unbearable."

Christina's smile faded. "Oh, what a shame."

"We think the problem is the fig tree." Gwen gestured to the offending plant. "The fruit attracts... animals." She'd almost said bugs and animals but thought better of it. No point in mentioning the roaches too.

"I have just the thing." Christina fumbled in her purse and pulled out a pack of gum. "Want a piece?"

Gwen gazed at the offering, a question in her eyes.

"My brother-in-law is a coroner. He swears by gum." She popped a piece in her mouth and chewed.

"I think we should reschedule." Gwen made her tone apologetic, but firm.

"Don't be silly." Christina waltzed past her toward the front door. "I'm not going to let a little bird stand between me and a sale." She disappeared inside.

Gwen stared at the empty stoop for a long moment, then followed. As soon as she entered the house, she wished she had taken that piece of gum.

1.3.7

ON FRIDAY AFTERNOON, Gwen's phone buzzed from somewhere under her desk. She followed the sound to her purse. She'd stowed it there when she arrived at the office.

"Hey." It was Lance.

"Hey, yourself. How's it going?"

"Well, it turned out the animal in the vent pipe was a rat, not a bird. That's why it smelled so terrible. The removal guy said rats are the worst."

"Nice," Gwen said with a shudder. Her dislike for rats was only second to her loathing of roaches.

"He hooked the thing and pulled it out with a rope. Then he sprayed it with a biological chemical. It was very interesting."

"I'm glad I wasn't there." Gwen grimaced. "How does the house smell now?"

"I aired everything out and burned a few candles. Smelled fine when I left."

"Thanks for handling that," Gwen said, her voice growing soft.

"Not a problem." Gwen heard a rustle of paper through the phone, then Lance said, "So what do you hear from that real estate agent?"

"Christina? She sent pictures to her clients, and they loved the house. She called to tell me this morning."

There was a long pause, then Lance said, "So, what are the next steps? Do we stop work?"

He sounded disappointed, and Gwen realized she felt the same. She enjoyed watching the depressing house transform under Lance's guidance. She enjoyed working with him. It would be difficult to stop midstream.

"No, not yet. She said she expected to have an offer for us soon, but I'm not going to say anything to Fiona until I see the whites of their eyes. It's easy to say you love something when you're looking at photos. It's entirely different when you're standing on site."

Lance exhaled. "Good. I'm halfway through the master bathroom, and I really want to finish."

"You're doing the tile yourself?" She was surprised by how much of the actual work Lance did. Many contractors only hired laborers and supervised.

"I like tiling, but I'm not going to do the other bathrooms. This one inspired me." He laughed. "Not often you find a tub with an ocean view."

"I know. It makes me want to sit in a mountain of bubbles with a glass of champagne and watch the sun set." As soon as Gwen said the words, she wished she hadn't. She'd imagined sitting in that tub alone or with Art, but that wasn't what she'd said. It would be natural for Lance to think she was flirting.

"I put in a new bathtub." He sounded excited. Not about her, though. About the job.

She relaxed. "Really? That in the budget?"

He spoke quickly. "I got a deal, and that old tub was bad. Couldn't get it clean anymore."

"I was teasing. It needed to be replaced," Gwen said.

"Wait until you see it," the excitement returned to his voice. "It's got jacuzzi jets."

Gwen opened her desk drawer, pulled out her calendar and made notes on their plans for the following week. She still used a paper planner, unlike Maricela and most of the other agents in the office. When you had to keep track of four schedules, it seemed easiest. Besides, she liked the feel of a pen in her hands.

When they exhausted the to-do list, they hung up and Gwen began straightening her desk and collecting her things. Today was Valentine's Day. She'd told Art she'd pick up the kids from school. Her plan was to shuttle them off to their evening's activities, race home, and surprise him with a picnic dinner around the fireplace.

She stood, shouldered her bag, and heard the familiar clink of keys. Not hers, which made almost no noise since the few metal keys she used were divided by her car remote. It was the set that opened the doors of the house on Cliff Drive.

She fished them from her bag, opened her desk drawer, moved to place them inside, but hesitated. When she had client keys—which wasn't all that often these days because of computerized lockboxes—she locked them in her desk when she wasn't using them.

But she couldn't remember ever locking this set up. Had she been carrying them around all week? Between the problems on Cliff Drive, running around after the kids, and planning tonight, she'd been distracted.

An image burst into her mind in technicolor—Don Gordon standing at her desk, contract in hand, her purse at his elbow. The keys to the house had been inside.

She blinked. So what? He hadn't had enough time to take the keys, make copies, and return them while she'd been in the bathroom.

Gwen set the keys down and closed the drawer, then paused again. Could he have taken them and returned them later in the day?

She reviewed the earlier part of the week. She'd gone to the house on Monday morning but hadn't returned until Thursday. It was possible he'd removed them Monday and put them back in her purse on Tuesday or Wednesday. Her purse would've been on or under her desk unattended any number of times.

Don Gordon was competitive and full of himself, but would he stoop so low as to plant cockroaches and rats in her listing?

I haven't heard about the cockroaches. His words rang through her mind. He'd encouraged Carolyn to tell her story last week at The Leaky Barrel. He'd seen Gwen's response; knew how repelled by the bugs she was.

Again, so what?

Half the agents from the office were there that same night. In her mind, she saw each laughing face as they sat around the high-top table—Maricela, Carolyn, Amelia, Robert. They were her friends. The only one she could imagine committing an act of sabotage was Don Gordon, and that was a big stretch.

She shook her head. He wouldn't do a thing like that. She was being paranoid, as Lance had said. She'd worked hard at overcoming the emotion, but it still haunted her from time to time.

After her parents' divorce, her life had slid down the economic ladder many rungs. Most of her clothing came from the second-hand stores and even the new things were never name brands. But it was about more than money. In retrospect, she saw that she'd worn the shame of her situation like a cloak. It attracted bullies like a matador's cape attracts bulls.

"Coming to the Barrel?" Carolyn's voice made Gwen jump.

"Oh." She put a hand on her chest.

"Didn't mean to scare you." Carolyn smiled mischievously as if she'd enjoyed it, though.

"No, I can't go tonight."

The grin faded from Carolyn's face. "That's right. It's Valentine's Day. You probably have a date with that handsome husband of yours."

"I do."

"You are a very lucky woman, Gwen Bishop." Carolyn turned her gaze toward two other female agents who were heading out the door. "See you Monday." She hurried after them.

Gwen was a lucky woman. She had a great husband, three terrific kids, and her business was doing well, so why was she so worried? Paranoid. The word was an uncomfortable fit.

She closed her eyes. Shake it off. She'd gotten rid of the bullies before; she could do it again. At ten, Alan Grossman had taught her how to fight. His father had taught him, and he passed on the wisdom to her.

It had worked. Girls scratched and pulled hair. Gwen had found that tackling and punching were more effective. By the time she turned twelve, the bullies had given her a wide berth.

All that was in the past, however. Today she was a lucky woman.

That was what she'd focus on. She pulled her own keys from her purse, placed the smallest one into the desk lock, and turned it.

There. Locked up tight. Everything was safe for the night. It was time to head home, put all this out of her head, and enjoy the evening with her husband.

1.3.8

GWEN HEARD the front door open and checked the clock. It was 7:15. Art was late. She'd expected him between 6:00 and 6:30, but swallowed her irritation. This was a surprise, so he hadn't known that, had he?

"Hey there." She patted the couch when he entered the living room.

Art dropped next to her and accepted the glass of wine she handed him. "You look nice." He pecked her on the cheek.

Not exactly the response she'd been hoping for when she put on the blue V-neck sweater he loved. The one he said made her eyes turn from brown to green. "The kids are gone." She shot him a flirty smile.

"Emily?"

"She's at Maricela's." Gwen set her glass down and wrapped her arms around his neck. "For the night." She kissed him.

Art returned the kiss, but it felt more perfunctory than passionate. He must need to settle in. She pulled back and picked up a plate. "Hungry?"

"What's all this?" He took the plate of food from her hand.

"Happy Valentine's Day."

A look of dismay crossed his face. "Oh, no. Gwen, I totally forgot—"

She cut him off with a wave of her hand. "I remembered for both of us."

He gave her a weak smile, set down his plate without tasting anything, and cradled his wine glass. The smile faded as quickly as it had come.

"How were things at school today?" Her voice sounded too bright.

"Not great." He lifted his glass and drank deeply.

Gwen sat up straighter. This wasn't going the way she'd hoped, but part of being a good spouse was listening and being compassionate. "What's going on?"

Art shook his head.

She took a long sip of wine, set down her glass, and pivoted to face him. This was her second, or maybe third, glass. It was time to slow down. She'd started drinking while she was waiting for him and had lost count. "Talk to me."

"It's Brian.'

Something cold dropped into Gwen's gut. *Brian? Really?* "Oh?"

"Well, it's the board. They're still talking about taking away his scholarship." His face hardened into angry lines. "If they do—"

He broke off and gulped his wine again. Gulped his Red Ravish. Gulped the expensive wine she'd splurged on to accompany their romantic Valentine's Day evening together.

"If they do, what?" She heard the frost in her own voice.

"I may have to resign." His words thudded on top of the wall that had been growing between them.

"Resign?"

He ran a hand over his head. "What else can I do?"

"You could take care of your own family." Gwen closed her eyes, willing the anger that was spreading through her like ice to halt. "I mean, it's just an option."

"Gwen." He said her name in that disappointed tone he used with the kids when they did something naughty.

The anger inside her flared. "No." She held up a hand. "Don't."

"Don't what?"

"Don't use that voice."

"I'm not—"

She cut him off. "I am not the one in the wrong this time."

"You're saying I am?"

"Yes. You are placing a higher priority on this... this... Olivia woman and her son than on your own family."

"No, I am not. It's merely a case of right and wr—"

"Crap on your right and wrong." Gwen grabbed her wine glass and downed the contents.

Art leaned back on the couch and glared at her. "Well, that was mature."

She inhaled and exhaled slowly. "I don't want to fight." She didn't. What she'd wanted was to talk about nothing, make out on the couch, and wind up in the bedroom.

"I don't either." His voice was soft.

"Then let's not." Gwen picked up his hand and wove her fingers through his. They sat that way, not speaking for a long moment, but it didn't stop her pulse from racing.

"I need to know I'm important to you," she finally said.

Art squeezed her hand. "Of course you are. You and the kids are the most important people in my life."

He'd said the words she'd wanted him to say. Then a half hour later, they made their way into the bedroom, and she was granted her second wish for the evening. So why did she feel empty as she lay in bed now, listening to him snore softly next to her?

Another bed on another night a long time ago filled Gwen's thoughts. Her father had come to her room to tuck her in after her mother's little birthday celebration. He'd kissed her forehead, smoothed her hair, and told her how special she was. She couldn't remember the last time he'd spoken to her so affectionately.

What came next taught her that words were cheap and easy. After her father had closed the door, Gwen burrowed under her covers with a flashlight and a book. She'd only read one chapter when she heard her parents' voices through the floor. Her mother's timbre was loud and piercing, her father's a low rumble.

She lay still for several minutes listening to the rise and fall of sound before throwing off her covers, making her way into the hall and perching at the top of the stairs.

What did they say about eavesdropping? No one ever heard anything good when they did? Gwen rolled over on her bed and punched her pillow. Why was this memory plaguing her tonight?

Crying won't do any good. I've made my decision. Her father's voice rang through her mind.

He'd made his decision. All by himself. Without asking anyone's opinion. It still amazed Gwen that he'd broken this news to his wife of fifteen years on her birthday.

How long has this been going on? Her mother had cried as she'd asked the question. Her father's response had been so flip, so dismissive. *It doesn't matter.*

That's what he'd said. *It doesn't matter.* As if the destruction of a family was nothing.

Gwen hadn't understood what they were talking about at the time, but a stab of primal fear had run through her anyway. Then her mother said something she did understand. She'd used the word abandonment.

Her father's response had been cold. I'm not the kind of man who shirks his responsibilities. But he had shirked his responsibilities. It was his responsibility to love, honor, and protect as well as provide.

Gwen pulled the covers up around her ears as if she could block out the voices of the past. Art wasn't anything like her father. She'd made sure of that before she'd married him. He was more than responsible. He cared. She squeezed her eyes shut, but sleep was a long time coming.

MOLLY: We're out of time, so we have to stop here. I just want to mention, that Gwen, like REK, didn't have the happiest of childhoods, but she didn't go around killing people.

This brings up the question of nature and nurture. Are our characters formed more from one or the other? Exclusively from one or the other? Or an equal combination of the two? What are your thoughts?

Let me know. The link is in the show notes. It'll be a good discussion to have as a prelude to the next episode. It's about to get darker, people.

Join me next time for more *Murders Under the Sun*.

(cue music)

VO: If you enjoyed this episode, please leave us a five-star review on your favorite podcast service—it really helps. *Murders Under the Sun* is edited by Jim Wilbourne, theme music is by Eclectic Blends, and I'm your host, Molly Shure.

part five

MURDERS UNDER THE SUN
   SEASON ONE; EPISODE FOUR

MOLLY: Welcome back to *Murders Under the Sun*. I'm Molly Shure, your host.

Before we get into today's show, I want to thank all you listeners for your kind words on social media and thanks, as well, to those who emailed. It's been a long time since I thought about Melissa, my old roommate. Talking about her did bring up some painful memories, as many of you believed.

And, how crazy was it that two of you have actually hung out at The Raven's Perch? I stopped going there after Melissa disappeared. It no longer felt safe to me. I'm sure there was nothing actually wrong with the bar. It just had the unlucky distinction of being the last place she was seen.

If the owners are listening, don't email me. I'm not maligning the place. It used to have a great happy hour and a DJ on Friday and Saturday nights. I've heard it's still a hot spot for CSU Fullerton students. Go Titans!

Alright, I'd better stop talking before I get myself in trouble. Let's dive into Gwen's story.

Warning, this episode begins with an entry from the Real Estate Killer that may be triggering for some. Don't listen with children or sensitive individuals present.

If you had any doubts about whether REK was evil or simply broken by his childhood, they'll be dispelled today. In my opinion, he is a true narcissist. I ran this opinion by a psychologist friend, and she agreed.

How are narcissists made? We asked the question: Is it nature, nurture or a combination of the two?

According to my research, most psychologists believe there is a genetic component. Certain personality traits come through the family line. But if genetics put the gun on table, early childhood experiences pull the trigger.

Both over-parenting and neglect can contribute to a narcissistic personality disorder. If a child can do no wrong, well, that's kind of obvious. But abuse and neglect can do as much, or even more, damage to a kid's psyche. Neglect, as we've learned through REK's journal entries, was his experience. However, as tragic as his childhood was, in my mind it doesn't absolve him of his crimes.

I'm done playing armchair psychologist, though. My job is to bring you the facts. Sometimes they're fascinating, sometimes puzzling, sometimes—like in today's episode—they're extremely disturbing.

1.4.2

THE VIEW WAS STUNNING—HER word, not mine. She stood in front of the large picture window and raised an upturned palm to the sparkling ocean beyond, like Vanna White offering a vowel.

"Million dollars, that's what it is." She smiled. The sunlight behind her turned her hair into a halo of gold. I took the vision as heavenly confirmation of the decision I'd already made. Gwen Bishop had pushed me to this. May it be on her golden head.

"Million dollars, at least," I agreed.

"Would you like to see the rest of the house?"

"Most definitely."

I followed her through the great room into an ocean of granite. She pointed out a breakfast nook, and down a short hall to a laundry room and maid's quarters. "Everybody Ought to Have a Maid," that old Broadway tune, played through my head.

She must have assumed cooking was beneath me because the kitchen only received a flap of her hand. I, however, recently discovered I wasn't too bad at slicing and dicing. An assortment of knives on a butcher's block caught my attention. I just had time to find one with a nice heft and pocket it before she rushed me onward.

The dining room was empty except for a chandelier as big as a freighter that marked where the table should go. The thought crossed my mind that I should kill her here, under that showstopper of a fixture. It would be so theatrical, so Hollywood. The setting should fit the crime and ostentatious was the word this wheel was spelling.

If there was ever a town that deserved that moniker, Newport Beach, California, was it. When Ms. White pulled up the paved drive in her powder blue BMW—vanity plate "HERBEEMR"—took her Louis Vuitton bag from the passenger seat, and graced me with her beautiful set of ivories, I almost laughed in her face.

She was another gorgon.

Another grasping chit.

Not even the abundance of makeup she wore could conceal her lust for status, her need for significance. The listing was just what you'd expect her to represent.

Ostentation was carved into the little-boy-peeing fountain in the front yard and the ivy scrollwork on the huge front doors. The word echoed through all the empty, cavernous rooms and swam in the infinity pool in the backyard. I hated it almost as much as I hated her. This would not be difficult.

The click of her heels on the hardwood floor grew softer. I had to hurry to catch up.

"The game room is really the best spot in the house, in my humble opinion," she said.

I doubted she considered any of her opinions humble.

She walked to the dead center of the space and spun toward me. Her beige skirt billowed. Her deceitfully pretty face devolved into a scowl when she noticed I had been lagging and almost missed the performance.

It was a fine room. Windows lined both west- and north-facing walls. You could see up the coast for miles. It reminded me of the living room in my beach house.

She was off, down a hall and halfway up the stairs, her non-stop talk trailing behind her like steam. "The master suite is directly above the game room. It is my second favorite space in the house. It has a fireplace, too, and the balcony is to die for."

Interesting choice of words. We toured the guest suites, none of which was very inspiring. Although my house needed attention, it had character. Much more character than this mini-mansion.

We descended another set of stairs into a wide hall. The first door led into a library. One wall was covered in floor to ceiling bookshelves, another with a heavy, mahogany-mantled fireplace.

The room was too Agatha Christie for my taste. Who-done-its aren't really about murder. They are about the cleverness of detectives, not something I was interested in thinking about at the moment.

After passing a sunroom and a music room, we walked into a theater. It was all done up in maroon and gold like an old-time cinema. There were no windows. The only light came from wall sconces that made long shadows of us as we marched toward the small stage. It was the perfect place to make a dramatic statement. I was glad I passed up the dining room.

"Amos Johnston, the man who commissioned the house, wanted this theater built for family performances as well as to watch movies — hence the stage," Ms. White informed. "His children were dancers and musicians."

"Do you dance?" I asked. My father's daughter—my half-sister, Fiona—danced in college. Something in the way this woman moved reminded me of her.

She spun toward me in a graceful pirouette. "Not really." Her voice faltered. "Well, that's about it. Only the garden left. We can exit at the end of the hall." She gestured the way we'd come.

"But I'd love to see you dance. Won't you climb onto the platform for me, Ms. White?"

"White? My name is Purcell, Christina Purcell."

"Yes, of course. It was only a joke."

"The exit is behind you." Her voice lost some of its refinement. A mid-western lilt lifted the final words of her statement.

I blocked her way. "The stage is behind you." I detected a whiff of fear hiding in the cloud of perfume floating around her.

"Now, this isn't funny, mister. I'm a married woman and not interested in any shenanigans."

Michigan or maybe Wisconsin? It's odd how people revert to the accents of their youth when they're afraid.

"But I love shenanigans." I took the knife from my jacket pocket and ran a finger over the blade.

MOLLY: It's hard to know what to say after reading that. So, I'm not going to say anything.

Let's get on with Gwen's story, and let her do the talking.

1.4.3

THE MONDAY after Valentine's Day, Gwen blew into the office to pick up her briefcase before heading to Dana Point to show a buyer a house that had recently come on the market. Maricela sat at her desk, unmoving.

Maricela was the most energetic person Gwen knew—a perpetual motion machine at work. Her uncharacteristic stillness brought Gwen to a stop; despite the fact she was running late.

"You okay?" she asked.

Maricela raised her eyes to Gwen's face. They were rimmed with red.

"What?" Gwen asked. "Is Julissa—"

"She's fine," Maricela said in a shaky voice. "They found another body."

The weight of Maricela's words took several seconds to fall. When they did, Gwen sat, her knees giving way.

"Who?"

"A Newport Beach agent. They found her in one of her listings."

"An accident?" Gwen asked without conviction.

Maricela gave her a withering gaze. "Right."

"What do the police say?"

"It's foul play. And she was found in an empty, ocean-view house."

Maricela's voice slid up the scale. "What do you want to bet her throat was cut?"

"Mari—"

"It's him. I know it."

"Him?" Gwen asked, but she knew who Maricela was referring to.

"Him," Maricela snapped. "The same guy who killed Sondra."

"We don't know that." Gwen used the tone she employed when her children had nightmares, calm and soothing.

"This one likes beach-front homes. The guy in Texas liked equestrian properties." She fixed her gaze on Gwen. "It's part of the fantasy for them. That's what the detective in Fort Worth told me."

A twister of emotions spiraled around Gwen, but she refused to focus on them. This wasn't happening. Not now. Not when she was so close to making a tremendous leap forward in her career.

She reached out a hand and squeezed her friend's arm. "Look, it's upsetting. It's bad. But forewarned is forearmed, right? We know someone might be out there. We can take precautions."

Maricela rested her head in her hands. "I'm scared. It feels personal."

"It's not. Nobody knows why this happened."

"It happened because there's a psycho targeting agents, just like in Texas." She shot Gwen a panicked gaze. "What if it's the same psycho? What if he decided he's sick of horses, and now he loves the beach?"

"No," Gwen's voice was decisive. "I don't believe that. We have no evidence that the crimes are connected."

Maricela gazed at her desktop without speaking for a long moment. Finally, she said, "You need to let go of that listing."

Gwen stared at her friend. She hadn't said which listing, but Gwen knew she meant Cliff Drive. "Why would I do that?"

"Because you might be next."

A jolt of adrenaline shot through Gwen. It could've been fear, but she chose to believe it was anger. She stood. She was sympathetic, but she didn't have to listen to this any longer. "That's crazy." She shouldered her purse but paused before walking out. "Are you still going to your support group?"

Maricela narrowed her eyes. "Really? Are you really asking me that?"

"I care about you."

"Let me tell you something, chica. Houses are like dogs. They're emotional vacuums. They absorb the love, the hate, the kindness, and the violence that happens inside them."

Gwen struggled for something to say to placate her friend. "I'll put motion sensor lights outside." The words sounded absurd, even to her own ears. "Will that make you feel better?"

Maricela uttered a low laugh. "You think lights will stop him?"

Gwen moved toward the door. She didn't want to hear the rest of Maricela's ravings. They might not be based in reality, but they were still unsettling.

Maricela's words trailed after her. "That house is poison, Gwen. I'm telling you."

Gwen crossed the parking lot and climbed into her Honda. She started the engine and placed her hands on the steering wheel. They were shaking.

Why? She didn't believe what Maricela had said. Her friend had PTSD. She'd been attacked, almost raped, in a vacant house. If another agent hadn't shown up without an appointment... The interruption had saved Maricela from things Gwen didn't want to think about.

She smacked the steering wheel. And that was the point. Maricela's close call had changed her forever. She lived, if not in fear, with extreme caution. She saw danger where there was none.

Gwen pulled out of her parking space. Poor Julissa was growing up with a helicopter hovering over her. It was amazing the child wasn't afraid of her own shadow.

As she made a left into traffic, she made a decision. She was Maricela's friend, and as a friend she would always support her. However, she couldn't allow Maricela's phobias to become her own, or how could she help her?

She merged onto the 5 Freeway, feeling calmer. Her phone rang a moment later. Lance's voice came through the car's speakers. "Hey, did you hear?"

"Hear what?" She said the words cautiously, hoping he was referring to a paint or plumbing problem.

"I guess our deal is dead." She heard an intake of breath. "Oh, gah. Terrible choice of words."

A needle of fear poked her. "What do you mean?"

"Christina Purcell, the agent who came by on Friday."

Gwen's hands began shaking again. She gripped the wheel tighter. "What about her?"

"You didn't hear?"

"Oh, for goodness sake, Lance," Gwen yelled at the dashboard of her car. "Just tell me what you're talking about."

There was silence for a long, terrible beat. "She's dead," he said. "Found with her throat cut in a vacant property in Newport." The silence returned, filling her car like a solid thing.

A minute later, a horn broke the stillness. She hadn't been paying attention to the road. The car sped around her. Startled, Gwen spun the wheel to the right. She slid into the slow lane, cutting off a pickup truck. Another horn blared.

She pulled onto the shoulder of the freeway, slowed to a stop, and rested her forehead on the hands that still held the steering wheel in a death grip.

Lance's voice entered the car again. "Gwen, where are you?"

"On the 5," she mumbled.

"Where?"

"Southbound, between Ortega and Camino Capistrano."

"Meet me at Hidden House Café in San Juan."

"I have an appointment in ten minutes."

"Afterward? Like ten-thirty?"

She inhaled deeply before answering. "Okay."

Another long beat, then Lance said, "You alright to drive?"

Two more inhales and exhales. "Yes."

They disconnected, and Gwen restarted her car. She drove in the slow lane past two more off ramps and exited onto the Coast Highway. She'd put her smile in place and show the property in Dana Point like a professional. Then she'd meet Lance in San Juan Capistrano and find out what the hell was going on.

1.4.4

GWEN skirted around the porch of the old building the coffee house was located within. Lance sat at an outside table, two steaming mugs in front of him. She slipped onto a cold metal chair across from him.

"You okay?" His eyes were filled with concern. "I shouldn't have sprung the news on you like that. I'm sorry."

"Maricela already told me an agent had died, but I didn't know it was Christina Purcell."

Lance pushed one of the mugs toward her. "I got you a latte."

"Thanks." Gwen took a sip. The heat was comforting. "What do we do?"

"Do?" He looked genuinely confused.

"Do we talk to Fiona?" At that moment, the idea of stepping foot into the Laguna house seemed an impossible task. He was still out there. The man who had turned Sondra Olsen into a lifeless, bloodied corpse was still out there.

Lance sipped his own drink slowly as if giving himself time to think of a response. "It would just upset her," he finally said.

"Of course it would upset her," Gwen said. "This is what she was afraid of."

"It was my understanding," Lance said, "that Fiona was afraid you'd be killed. Or that someone else would be killed in the house on Cliff Drive. Christina Purcell was killed in Newport Beach."

Gwen waved away his words. "But she was about to bring in an offer."

"Nobody knew that." He tipped his head to one side. "Unless you told someone."

Gwen shot him a look. "No. Nobody."

"Not Fiona?"

"No. I told you I planned to wait until we had an offer in hand."

Neither of them spoke for a long moment. Gwen broke the silence. "You didn't—"

"No." He interrupted her. "That's your side of the business. Not mine.

Throughout her appointment that morning, she'd tried to convince herself the Laguna property was safe. That she was safe. She'd told herself that, statistically, she was the most unlikely person to become a victim since lightning didn't strike twice in the same place.

Unless, of course, a person lived next to a lightning rod. That thought had occurred to her as she'd said goodbye to her clients and locked the home they'd just toured. Honestly, the only person who still lived by the buddy-system was Maricela. It just wasn't practical.

On the drive to the coffee shop, she'd begun to wonder if Maricela were right and the home had absorbed something that now attracted evil. That maybe the house on Cliff Drive was, in fact, a lightning rod.

This was her frame of mind as she'd sat at the table across from Lance. But he'd just made a very good point. If nobody knew about the pending offer, then how could Christina's death be connected to the property? The sense of doom Gwen had been suffering under began to lift.

"Listen," Lance said. "This is a terrible tragedy, but we hardly knew the woman."

Gwen inhaled. The air smelled of sage and horses. The guy in Texas liked equestrian properties. This one likes beach-front homes. Maricela's words rang in her mind. "What if it's the same murderer?"

"He'd definitely be someone who hates real estate agents." Lance's tone was droll.

Another thought struck Gwen. "Or someone in the business. Someone pathologically competitive."

Lance sat back in his chair. "That's a dark idea."

A dry, scented breeze blew Gwen's hair into her face. She pushed the strands away and tucked them behind an ear. Were these crimes of convenience? A predator who'd discovered real estate agents were easy prey. Or was there more to it?

"I think we should go to the police," she said. "The fact that both Sondra and Christina were connected to the house is too coincidental."

He nodded his head slowly. "You're right, but..."

"But what?"

"There are only a handful of people who knew about that connection, which means they'll all come under scrutiny."

Gwen blinked. "You don't think they'd suspect me?"

He lifted a shoulder and let it drop. "More likely, they'll suspect me."

"But you weren't even around when Sondra died."

"I live and work in Orange County. They'll investigate me."

The day suddenly seemed cold. Gwen held her mug with both hands, relishing the warmth. "And they won't find anything."

"Right." He stood, a look of resignation on his handsome features. "Ready?"

She downed the rest of her coffee and rose. "Let's go."

Gwen's first impression of Detective Sylla was that she was young—too young to be an investigator. But as she made her way toward them, small crow's feet around her dark eyes became visible. Her build and athletic stride had created the image of youth. She was slender, but well-muscled, with skin so uniformly dark it looked like polished ebony against her white shirt.

After introductions, she led Gwen and Lance down a hallway to an interview room with green walls and a rickety-looking table surrounded by four plastic chairs.

"How can I help you?" she said as they took seats across from each other at the long table. Her accent was British. Gwen wondered what her story was. How had a Brit ended up in the Orange County Sheriff's Department? She'd probably never know.

Sylla cleared her throat, a not-so-subtle reminder of what they were there for.

"We have information that may pertain to the, ah..." Gwen couldn't seem to make herself say death or killing or, worse yet, murder.

"The death of the real estate agent in Newport," Lance filled in.

Sylla's eyebrows rose, but she didn't speak.

Gwen rallied. "Christina Purcell was going to bring in an offer on my listing."

Still Sylla didn't speak, but Gwen had the distinct impression she felt they were wasting her time. "We thought it might be significant because of the home's history," Gwen said.

"History?" The detective sounded bored.

Lance leaned forward and rested his arms on the table. "Sondra Olsen was killed in the house."

Now they had Sylla's attention. Her eyes grew wide, and her spine straightened. "The house on Cliff Drive in Laguna?"

"Yes," Gwen said.

"Fiona Randall recently decided to list it again," Lance said.

Detective Sylla's gaze moved to his face. "And what exactly is your position in all this, Mr. Fairchild?"

"I'm a general contractor. Fiona hired me to make improvements on the property before putting it back on the market."

"I hadn't heard it was available for sale again." Sylla looked thoughtful.

Gwen shook her head. "It isn't. Not yet."

Sylla furrowed her smooth forehead in an unspoken question. Gwen filled her in on the timeline of events: signing the listing, Christina's visit to the house, and then her call, telling Gwen that she expected to have an offer from her clients on the property any day.

When she finished, the detective asked, "Is that usual? Making an offer on a house one has never seen?"

"No," Gwen said. "It's very unusual, but Christina said her buyers lived out of state. She sent them pictures."

"Do you have contact information for them?"

"I don't. I never saw an offer."

Sylla stared at the wall behind Gwen for a long beat before saying, "Who else knew about it?"

"I don't know." Gwen shrugged. "The only person I spoke to was Lance."

"Not the owner? Fiona Randall?" Sylla asked.

"No. I didn't want to get her hopes up if it fell through."

"We don't know who Christina Purcell told, though." Lance spoke a little too quickly, and Sylla's gaze slid toward him.

A twinge of discomfort went through Gwen. *They'll investigate me.* Lance's earlier words may prove to be true. "We don't know if this has anything to do with Christina's death." She forced the word out. "But it seemed like it might. Two agents, both with a connection to the same property."

Sylla asked one or two more questions neither Gwen nor Lance knew the answers to, then rose. "I appreciate you coming forward."

Gwen and Lance followed her into the hallway. When they reached the lobby, Sylla turned to face them, eyes on Lance. "Where can I reach you if we have more questions?"

Gwen handed her a business card. Lance did the same, and they left. As the two crossed the parking lot to their vehicles, Gwen had a sudden urge to put this entire thing behind her. The house no longer seemed the boon she'd once believed it to be. It felt like a liability.

She spun toward Lance. "Is there any chance we can hold an open house this weekend?"

Lance stopped at the tailgate of his truck. "There's a lot left to do, but maybe. If I can pull in some extra guys. What are you thinking?"

"I don't want to abandon Fiona, but I want out of this thing."

"I get that, but there's a lot of money at stake." He leaned against the truck as if settling in for a conversation. "For all of us."

The sun was shining, but Gwen felt cold. She wrapped her arms around herself. "When that detective calls Fiona, she'll be tempted to mothball the house for another three or four months."

"Or…" Lance looked thoughtful. "She may lower the price, list it way under market, just to get rid of it quickly."

That didn't sound like a terrible idea to Gwen. "She might."

"That wouldn't be good for either one of us." The lines of Lance's face hardened when Gwen didn't respond. "It's not only the money. It's also my reputation. And yours."

"Mine?"

"How is it going to look if you sell a house like that for a fraction of what it's worth?"

"But, Sondra—"

Lance put up a hand to stop her words. "Most people have already forgotten about that."

"Detective Sylla knew exactly who you were talking about."

"She's police. Of course she remembers. I'm talking about the future, about potential clients who look at your track record to decide if they want to list with you." His voice grew angry. "Or my potential clients, who see I never finished this house."

"Under the circumstances, I think they'd give us both a pass."

"But they won't remember the circumstances."

The wind tugged at Gwen's sweater. She pulled it tighter around herself. "So what are you suggesting?"

"I'm suggesting we create a united front when Fiona starts to panic."

Gwen searched his eyes for the steel she heard in his voice, but all she found there was concern. "Then, I'll ask you again. Can we hold the open house on Saturday?"

His gaze skittered around the parking lot as if seeking an answer there. It finally came to rest on his feet. "Can you help?"

"Sure. What do you want me to do?"

"Keep Fiona from making a hasty decision?"

"No promises, but I can try."

"Shop? Get a few decorator items?"

"That I can do."

His eyes returned to her face. "Alright, then. Let's make it happen."

1.4.5

THE NEXT DAY, Gwen and Maricela wandered through an antique mall in downtown San Juan Capistrano looking for things to dress up their listings. Gwen held up a ceramic Toreador lamp topped by a frolicking bull lampshade. "You could do a Tijuana theme."

"Or I could shoot myself," Maricela said. "We're going tropical. Rosie—she's the decorator my clients hired—said the colors should remind people they're close to the beach. She's really good. You should talk to her about the Laguna property."

"We don't have time for an interior designer. Our goal is to finish the projects Lance has already started, then downplay the house and focus attention on the views. I just need a couple of vases. Fresh flowers cover a multitude of sins."

"I wonder what's in here?" Maricela stood at the open door of a storage room stuffed floor to ceiling with merchandise. Chairs and tables were piled one on top of another, dimming the light from overhead bulbs.

Gwen pointed to a "sale" sign with an arrow directing buyers inside.

"Let's check it out." Maricela disappeared down a narrow path between mountains of furniture.

"I'll wait here," Gwen called after her.

"Be right back." Her voice echoed from the doorway.

Gwen browsed the booths near the entrance until Maricela returned with two vases, one crystal, one milk glass. "What about these?"

"Perfect."

As they moved away from the sale section, Maricela said, "Chica, what's with you and tight places?"

"Not sure what you mean." Gwen stopped at a section filled with dishes. She held up two bowls. "What do you think of these? You could fill them with seashells for the coffee table—kinda tropical."

"Nice." Maricela took them from Gwen. "But don't change the subject."

"I have a touch of claustrophobia, that's all." Gwen said.

"A touch? You wouldn't try on that skirt at the mall because the changing room was too small."

"It was too small. And it was dark."

"What exactly are you afraid of?" Maricela asked.

Gwen stopped mid-aisle to look at a stained-glass lamp. It would look lovely in the window of the dining room, but then she'd have to get a table to set it on.

"Gwen." Maricela's voice grew sharp. "What are you afraid of?"

Gwen snapped her head toward her friend. "Bugs. Okay? I don't like bugs."

A small smile played around the edges of Maricela's mouth. "Bugs? That's it?"

"You have irrational fears. I have irrational fears." As soon as she said the words, she regretted them. Bugs and rapists weren't at all the same thing. She opened her mouth to apologize, but Maricela had spun on her heel and was already walking away from her.

By the time she caught up, her friend was looking at a pile of throw pillows. "These are nice."

Gwen was relieved. Maricela was going to let her insensitivity go. The ability to forgive one another was probably why they'd been friends for so long since neither one was the most tactful person on the planet.

She was about to comment on the pillows when her phone vibrated. She pulled it out of her purse and smiled at the screen. "Lance needs me to pick up another ceiling light. I'll have to stop at Home Depot."

"Hmmm...," Maricela said.

They wandered a bit farther. Gwen could tell Maricela was itching to say something. Several times, she opened and closed her mouth as if she were considering then discarding words the way she was the items on the shelves.

"Okay, what's the problem?" Gwen asked when she couldn't take it any longer.

"What do you mean?" Maricela turned to her with wide eyes.

"I'm sorry I made the irrational fear comment."

"What irrational fear comment?"

She knew very well which comment. It was her way of letting Gwen know that wasn't what she was upset about. "Then what?"

Maricela toyed with a candlestick she'd picked up. "Art is a good husband," she said after a long pause.

Gwen laughed. "That's it?"

"I don't think you appreciate how few good husbands are out there these days."

Maricela set the candlestick down and moved toward the counter at the front of the store. Gwen remembered her earlier warnings about Lance, and her face flushed with annoyance.

After they made their purchases and emerged into the sunshine, Gwen turned to face Maricela. "There's nothing romantic going on between Lance and me. We have a business relationship. That's it."

"I made you mad. I'm sorry," Maricela said simply.

Instead of accepting, Gwen headed toward the car. Maricela didn't look sorry at all.

"Lance is a player, you know?" Maricela said.

"No, I don't know." Gwen heard the frost in her own voice.

"He uses people. I know his type."

"Oh, you do?"

"Yes, I do. I was married to one."

They got in Gwen's Honda and drove in silence. Gwen didn't know what to say. Maricela meant well, but she was wrong. Lance was secure in who he was. He was confident. She didn't know if he'd had a fling with the wife of a former client or not, but she knew he was nothing like Maricela's ex who bedded women to boost his tiny ego. She couldn't defend him, however. It would only make Maricela surer there was something going on between them.

Ten minutes later, they reached the office. Gwen parked, turned off the engine, and reached for the door handle, but Maricela put a hand on her arm. "I think Art is stressed about school."

Irritation tightened Gwen's jaw. Art was responsible for getting a partial scholarship for Julissa when Maricela had first moved to Orange County, before she'd gotten her business up and running. In Maricela's mind, he could do no wrong.

She didn't understand the reality of living with a man who made responsibility an art form. A man who was every forgotten mom's hero —except hers. It seemed the stronger and more self-reliant Gwen became, the less interest she held for him.

She wanted to tell her friend she wasn't the distracted one.

She'd planned a romantic evening. She'd tried to reconnect, to celebrate their marriage, on Valentine's Day. But she couldn't say any of that. It would be disloyal.

"I'm stressed, too," she said instead and threw open the car door.

Maricela looked at her. "I think you're being unfair."

"To whom?"

"To Art. I heard he and the board aren't seeing eye to eye on things."

Gwen exited the car and strode across the blacktop toward the office. Maybe the board was right this time. But she couldn't say that either.

She and Maricela worked side by side for several hours without the usual banter. Gwen threw herself into paperwork, ignoring the office noise and her hurt feelings.

"Hmm," a deep voice startled her. "That must be riveting." Don Gordon nodded at the mountain of papers on her desk.

"Fascinating." Gwen nodded.

"Is your Laguna house in escrow yet?" he asked.

"No." Gwen's voice was flat. He was always fishing, but it wasn't any of his business.

"I may have an interested party." Don thumped her desk with his forefinger.

"I'd like to take a look at it before I show it."

"We're having an open house on Saturday," Gwen said, keeping her eyes on her paperwork in the hopes of ending the conversation. She didn't feel like talking. Not to him, anyway.

"Will you be there?" he asked.

Gwen looked up in surprise. "Yeah, of course."

"Good. I'm interested to hear your sales pitch." His smile made him look like a ferret.

She opened a desk drawer, rummaged around and pulled out a piece of paper. "Here's the flier," she said. "Everything you need to know in four colors."

"Oh, okay. Thanks." The smile faded. He started to walk away but turned again. "Is there a lockbox?"

"Not an official one, not until it's actually on the market."

He nodded and strode to his desk without another word. Gwen and Maricela looked at each other, and Maricela rolled her eyes. They went back to work, the air between them warmer. Nothing like uniting over a common enemy to heal a rift.

Another hour passed, and Gwen's stomach growled. She looked at her watch. It was 12:30. Maricela's words about Art had been niggling at her like a splinter all morning. She didn't actually believe the board was correct in the case of Brian McKibben. As annoying as it was, her husband was in the right.

She sighed. She was still angry about the other night. That was her problem, and she needed to get over it.

She made a quick decision, stood, and grabbed her purse. She'd head to school and take him to lunch even if she had to drag him.

1.4.6

GWEN FOUND herself in the hall outside Art's office and hesitated with her hand on the knob. What was she hoping for? That his face would light up when he saw her? That he would drop everything, go with her to lunch then home for a quick dessert like he used to? Nostalgia ached in her chest.

This wasn't about her, however. It was about him. Art was going through a hard time. She was there to show her support.

Yes, a part of her wanted to curl up in his lap and tell him about Christina Purcell's death and her visit to the police station. She'd love to blubber all her fears and disappointments out on his shoulder, but now wasn't the time.

Honestly, she knew what his response would be anyway. He'd tell her to cancel the contract, and that wasn't going to happen. Gwen pushed open the door.

Millie sat at her desk in the front room, as she had for the past thirty years. She'd become as much a part of the school as the statue of St. Barnabas standing in the courtyard. Her hair was steel gray, her skin like dark leather, and she was as intractable as her appearance. Nobody messed with Millie. When she saw Gwen, she smiled.

"Hi, Millie," Gwen said.

"He's not here. I'm sorry."

When Millie referred to Art as "Him" or "He," it always sounded as if she used a capital "H," like there were no other "hims" or "hes" worth talking about. Yet another woman who adored her husband.

"Oh, well, it was nothing important. I had some free time."

"How is everyone doing at home?" Millie asked. "I've been concerned about Him."

"We're fine. Art's fine."

"I'm not sure He is." Millie's face became solemn. "He hasn't been Himself ever since Brian McKibben's accident."

"He takes responsibility for everything that happens at St. Barnabas, whether he should or not," Gwen said.

"Yes." Millie nodded her head sagely. "And it's hard to get through to Him when he blames Himself for things that aren't His fault."

His fault. Was the accident his fault? Certainly not directly. Gwen tried to put herself in his shoes, but she couldn't. She wasn't built like him. Once she made a decision, she'd made it. If the outcome wasn't what she'd hoped, she made plans to fix the problem. She didn't wallow.

"It's great to be a person of character, but you can't take the weight of the world on your shoulders," she said because Millie seemed to be expecting a response.

"Exactly," Millie agreed. "But you know what He's like."

Yes, Gwen knew all too well, and because of that, she needed to find him. "Do you know where he is?"

"He said he was going to Enzo's to grab a slice of pizza for lunch."

Enzo's parking lot was full with lunch crowd vehicles. Gwen circled several times before she remembered there were spaces behind the building. She cut between the restaurant and a florist shop into a service alley and parked next to a VW Bug with a pizza-shaped flag attached to its passenger-side window.

She picked her way around cast-off cardboard boxes and stacks of pallets back toward the alley she'd driven through. The bright sunlight dimmed as she walked into the shade. It took her eyes a moment to adjust.

A few yards in, she saw a door opened to the alley. It must be the restaurant's rear exit. As she drew closer, she heard murmurs coming from the doorway—a man's voice, low and pleading, a woman crying.

Gwen stopped, not wanting to intrude on what sounded like a lover's quarrel. She stood in indecision, wondering if there were another path around the building, or if she should clear her throat and let the couple know someone was coming. Before she could do either, they came into view.

The woman was petite, blond, and attractive, even with mascara tracks decorating her cheeks. She was dressed in black jeans and an Enzo's t-shirt. She looked familiar. It was a moment before Gwen recognized her in the uniform. The man's back was to her, but she had no trouble recognizing him.

It was Art.

The woman was Olivia Richards, Brian's mother.

What the hell was Art doing in an alley with one of his student's mothers? She couldn't hear their conversation, but based on the emotion on the woman's face and her tears, it was intense and personal.

Neither of them had noticed Gwen, so she stepped behind a dumpster located against the wall of the flower shop. She needed a minute to process.

Art. In an alley. With another woman.

Was Art having an affair after all? She put a hand to her chest and covered her heart. Even though the thought of him cheating had teased around in her brain once or twice when she was having a dark day, Gwen hadn't taken her fears seriously. Not really. Seeing her husband with another woman didn't compute. It was surreal. He was a good man. Everyone said so.

This woman did make a weird kind of sense, however. Art liked to be the hero. He loved to champion the cause of the underdog. If he were to be tempted into adultery, it would most likely be disguised by a virtuous cause—a damsel in distress. Based on the emotions echoing through the alley, this damsel qualified.

Think, Gwen. Think.

Her hand moved from her chest to her forehead and massaged her temples. She'd spent the ten minutes it had taken her to drive here berating herself for being self-centered, for not being understanding or sympathetic enough. It had been a very uncomfortable ten minutes. She didn't want to repeat them.

Gwen had no idea why Art was in deep conversation with Olivia Richards in an alley. Maybe the doctors had given her bad news. Maybe the board had officially and finally cancelled Brian's financial support. The point was, there were any number of scenarios that would cover the scene before her. Why assume the worst?

Gwen's hand dropped to her side, and she straightened her spine. She would step out from behind the dumpster and greet them as if nothing were wrong. Because as far as she knew, nothing was. Think the best. Believe the best. Wasn't that biblical? She'd step out and...

How would she explain why she was hiding behind a dumpster?

She slumped against the wall of the florist shop and stared at her feet. The sound of Art's voice rose and fell. She caught a word here and there: "sorry," "my fault," "important to me," "anything for you." It was that last phrase, "anything for you," that revived her fears.

She and Art used to perform a little stand-up routine, a private vaudeville shtick, when they were feeling romantic. Art would say, "I was so stuck on you, baby, I'd have done anything for you. Anything in the world to make you mine."

Gwen would respond, "Too bad I didn't know that when you asked me to marry you. I'd have held out for more than a half carat and a honeymoon in Mexico."

They hadn't had that conversation in years.

The odor of rotting flower stems permeated the air. The smell raised the ghost of another day. It had been a Friday afternoon. She'd perched on the front steps outside her mother's small apartment, her pink Barbie suitcase by her side. She'd been there a long time. It was her Dad's weekend, and he was late.

Again.

As she'd sat, a thought struck her. Her parents' divorce must be her fault. At first, she'd blamed her father's new wife. She'd hated Jenny with a hatred so pure only a child could manufacture it. But what if the problem had been Gwen all along?

Her father had often reprimanded her for being whiny, a complainer. Even after the terrible incident with the cockroaches, he'd laughed and told her to toughen up. If Gwen had only kept her problems to herself, their family might still be together.

The sun set. The streetlights came on. Gwen waited. The longer she sat, the longer her repentance speech became. She couldn't wait to tell him how sorry she was, how she would change.

It must have been past suppertime—her stomach was rumbling—when her mother eased herself onto the stoop next to her. Gwen's dad wasn't going to make it. Something had come up.

In the months that followed, something came up more and more often, until Gwen stopped feeling the ache of disappointment.

Three years after they broke up, Gwen's father and Jenny had a child on the way. Gwen's mother was drowning in gin. And Gwen had learned the devastation divorce could bring.

That day on the stoop when she'd had her epiphany, there had been a trash can nearby in which someone had dumped an old bouquet. Smell, strong emotion, and memory occupied close territory in the brain. The scent of decaying vegetation had linked arms with regret, fear, and a sense of abandonment and trotted into her neural pathways. The irony of that odor being present now wasn't lost on her.

The alley had grown quiet while she'd visited the past. Gwen realized she hadn't heard Art's voice or the woman's sobs for several minutes. Maybe they'd gone inside the restaurant, and she could escape unnoticed.

She longed for time alone to figure all this out. She pushed herself off the wall and crept to the edge of the dumpster. The noise of her heels on concrete sounded like drumbeats in the dead air.

She peered into the alleyway where she'd first seen Art and the woman, expecting it to be vacant. But they were there, spotlighted by a patch of sunlight. Art's arms enveloped the woman. Her face was buried in his chest. They stood in a silent embrace.

MOLLY: Poor Gwen. This is rough. Not only is she dealing with all the stuff at the Cliff House and the murder of Christina Purcell, but now she's wondering what's going on with Art and Olivia.

What do you all think? Are the two of them having a fling? Art seems like such a great guy, but even great guys have their weaknesses. On social media, we'll be talking about that, about the second murder, and what you'd do if you were in Gwen's shoes.

In the next episode, things are going to come to a head for her. You don't want to miss it. We'll finally learn, along with Gwen, the identity of REK.

Join me next time for more *Murders Under the Sun*.

(cue music)

VO: This episode is brought to you by Pacific Financial, trusted investment advisors for over a decade. *Murders Under the Sun* is edited by Jim Wilbourne, theme music is by Eclectic Blends, and I'm your host, Molly Shure.

part six

MURDERS UNDER THE SUN
SEASON ONE; EPISODE FIVE

MOLLY: Welcome back to *Murders Under the Sun*. I'm Molly Shure, your host.

If you're just tuning in to the podcast today, I suggest you go back to Episode One and catch yourself up. However for those of you who've been on board from the beginning, I thought it was time to do a little recap.

What do we know so far?

We know a lot more than Gwen Bishop did at this point thanks to the Real Estate Killer's manuscript. We know he is the illegitimate son of the original owner of the cliff house and half-brother to Fiona Randall, the present owner. We know he'll stop at nothing, not even murder, to gain access to the treasure in the basement—whatever that is. We also know, he's without a conscience and totally dangerous.

What we don't know is who he is. Gwen has given us a few possibilities, people she suspects. He could be Don Gordon, fellow real estate agent. Don is competitive and hasn't wanted her to take the listing from the very beginning.

He could be Lance. As much as she likes him, she doesn't know much about him other than what Maricela has told her and that's not complimentary.

He could be a total stranger.

Today is the day we finally learn his identity along with Gwen. But I want to take a moment before we dig into the episode to thank her for her vulnerability. She didn't have to be as transparent with me as she was. So, why did she reveal all?

I'll give you her answer. Gwen wanted you, the listeners, to know what actually happened during the events that dominated the news cycle at the time. There are two reasons for this. The first is to clear her name. She was vilified by the press. Did she make mistakes? Absolutely. But not all the mistakes she was accused of.

The other reason for her transparency was compassion. "If one listener is saved from upending their life by my story, it's worth telling." Those were her words.

Those are almost the same words I expressed to you all when asked why I do what I do. Violence changes you.

When Mel disappeared, I went into seclusion for a time. I hid myself away, just me and my laptop. I researched everyone she knew. I looked at her friends, her boyfriends, her family. If the police couldn't find her, I was determined that I would.

Well, you know how that turned out. All my digging did was alienate me from the people who loved her most. It was a terrible time.

When I got past it, I realized, like Gwen, I wanted to make my trauma count for something.

Back to the episode. Let's hear from REK.

1.5.2

I SAT in my car in front of the house on Cliff Drive with my windows rolled down and waited for the darkness. A strong breeze blew off the ocean, and the palm trees at the end of the block bent toward the hills.

Today, I learned that Gwen is having an open house tomorrow. She is a force to be reckoned with. Honestly, I'm not sure what to do about her. Christina Purcell's demise didn't work. There are few options left.

Gwen may look like my sister, but she doesn't have Fiona's conniving intelligence. I've always suspected Fiona knows about me and is playing a game of cat and mouse. She is a manipulator of men.

My father was wrapped around her little finger. I'm sure she is the reason I wasn't mentioned in his will. I understand I was an embarrassment, but once he was dead, what was there to be embarrassed about? Who would care? And then, there is the treasure in the basement. Surely, he'd had me in mind when he left it untouched. I'm convinced he would have given me an inheritance if it weren't for Fiona.

I bumped into her by accident one day. I knew it was she even though I'd only seen her from a distance. Her photo had been in the local society section of the paper when her engagement was announced. Fiona, of course, didn't notice me.

She was coming out of a department store in Fashion Island, loaded down with bags—probably shopping for her upcoming nuptials. The date was drawing near.

I had the reaction most people have when they see a celebrity. I stopped and stared, then doubted my eyes. It was difficult to believe we were occupying the same few feet of space. We lived in such different worlds.

She, the beloved. I, the rejected. She, a part of my father's household. I, thrown off his property. She was the north pole of a magnet and I, the south. When I found myself in her field, the pull was irresistible.

I followed her past a fountain, down a row of boutiques, and into a coffee shop. I slipped behind her in line and inhaled her expensive perfume. I listened to the lilt of her voice and felt the warmth of the smile she bestowed on the barista. She was so confident, so happy.

A diamond—three-and-a-half or four carats—sparkled on her left hand. It was beautiful. She was beautiful.

Even I fell under her spell that day. I couldn't get her out of my mind. At first, I only followed her on social media. I attended her wedding on Instagram, then her honeymoon. When the flurry of photos subsided, I began to follow her car.

I trailed her from the dance school where she worked to her house. Once I knew where she lived, I would show up on the street whenever I could. In this way, I learned where she shopped, worked, ate, and played. On five different occasions, I drove behind her to our father's house in Laguna Beach.

And this brings me to my point: She came and went freely from this house for thirty-some-odd years. Now, it is my turn.

But I need time. Time to remove the treasure and—although it breaks my heart—to sell it. Then, I can buy the home that should've been mine by rights.

Even though the idea that I must purchase my own house galls me, I don't see another way forward. If I kill her, the property would go to one of our cousins. Who knows what they would do with it? They might move in.

Fiona is taunting me. She doesn't care about the house. This is all a game to her, but she will see that two can play. And when I compete, I win. All of that to say, the open house is not going to happen.

Streetlights popped on up and down Cliff Drive. The sun had set while I'd sat reminiscing. It was now dark enough for my errand. An older couple with a little thing on a leash that looked more guinea pig than dog strolled down the block. I waited until they turned the corner.

I hefted the black bag from the passenger seat and exited the car. The sound of the door closing behind me echoed down the quiet street. I looked around but didn't see anyone. I calmed myself with the thought that people in this neighborhood were used to the noise of late-night parties and tourists.

The past few days had been a roller coaster of emotions. I was on an ecstatic high after my adventure in Newport Beach. Everything had gone flawlessly. Then, imagine my dismay when I learned Gwen was planning an open house, as if nothing had happened. I'd been so sure Christina's death would take her down, that she'd run away and never look back. Gwen has more strength than I knew she possessed. More than *she* knew she possessed.

I'd had to come up with a new, more intimate plan. My mind spun in a hundred directions. I wanted Gwen to wonder if a corporeal being was behind these attacks, or if they were some trick of the house itself. Had the structure drawn cockroaches like a corpse draws maggots? Had it trapped a small rodent in its stovepipe like a carnivorous plant captures an unsuspecting bird? I smiled at my own cleverness as I reached for the gate.

Light. Bright. Blinding. I was caught.

I spun around, naked and exposed, in the glare of the spotlight. Any moment I expected the shriek of a siren.

But nothing came. When the pounding of my heart calmed, I heard crickets chirping again. The blood cleared from behind my eyes, and I saw the source of the light. There were three motion sensor lamps hidden in the foliage of the front yard, positioned to illuminate the entrance.

I cursed under my breath. Gwen may have installed a camera as well. Apparently, I wasn't the only spy.

I moved into the shadows and stood very still. In a few minutes, the lights clicked off. I thought I'd been angry when I'd heard my efforts hadn't stopped the wheels of progress, but it was nothing compared to the rage surging through me now. This was war.

MOLLY: I feel like I keep saying this, but that was chilling. If what REK has done up until now wasn't war, I'd hate to see what war is. But, people, we are going to see it. War is exactly where we're headed.

What you're about to hear are some of the most upsetting segments of this story. They're not for the faint of heart.

Let's move on to Gwen's perspective.

1.5.3

GWEN GOT to Laguna early on Saturday morning. She hadn't slept well since Tuesday, when she'd seen Art and Olivia hugging in the alley.

The morning was cool. Fog covered the ocean and scented the air with salt and seaweed. Gwen hoped it would burn off before the open house got underway. She popped her trunk and lifted out a bag of pillows and throws. The throw on top was one Art had bought her for a Christmas present. The soft fabric grated on her.

She'd planned to confront Art about what she'd seen that evening. But he'd come home late, deflated and exhausted. He hadn't acted like a man who was cheating.

Of course, she wasn't sure what a man who was cheating acted like. Her father had pulled the wool over her and her mother's eyes for six months. She'd been a child, but her mother had been a grown woman. People often don't see what they don't want to see. Could she be blinding herself?

She pushed open the gate and stopped, surprised. She closed it and opened it again. No squeak. She swung it back and forth several more times and broke into a grin. Good job, Lance. It was one of the final items on her list. At least he cared what she thought.

As she trudged toward the front door, the scene around the dinner table on Wednesday evening played through her mind. She'd poked at

Art like a doctor checking for nerve damage. Instead of using a needle, she used potentially painful questions. How was Brian doing? Had the board come to a final decision about next year's scholarship? How was Olivia holding up?

Art had answered each without so much as a flush on his cheeks. Brian wasn't out of the woods, but the doctors saw improvement. The scholarship didn't look good, but he was still fighting the good fight. Olivia was a trooper.

So why was she crying on his chest?

Gwen dropped the bag on the stoop, retraced her steps and pulled a bucket of fresh flowers from the back of the car. She very much hoped today would be a success. It had been a rotten week.

As the days had gone by, she'd felt more and more awkward about admitting to Art that she'd been in the alley. He'd want to know why she hadn't announced her presence, and she couldn't answer that. She wasn't sure she knew herself. The whole thing had gotten so tangled in her gut she didn't know how to unravel it.

So, she'd stayed silent and left the house as often as possible when he was there. It was no way to live. She knew she'd have to confront the situation at some point. But now, with all that was happening here at the house, it didn't seem the right time. She didn't have the emotional bandwidth.

Gwen fumbled with the new lockbox, entered the house, and hurried through the entryway, past the baleful basement door, into the kitchen. While she ran water into the vases she'd bought in San Juan, she pulled flowers from the bucket. Instead of fully staging the house, she and Lance had decided to use some of the furniture he'd found in a basement room, some odds and ends from her home, and flowers to make the place as homey as possible.

Gwen refused to go down to the cellar with him, so she had to trust his judgment. He did okay. An old sofa table with claw-foot legs sat in front of the picture windows in the living room gleaming with polish. Gwen glanced across the expanse of the floor before crossing to it.

No bugs.

No dead rats.

No surprises.

She set a vase of yellow tulips on the table. It made a striking contrast to the blue of sky and sea beyond.

A square wood table, gray with age, now sat between two black, ladder-back chairs under an ancient crystal chandelier in the dining room. The arrangement of white hydrangeas and roses with celery green grass would look elegant against the severe backdrop, she decided.

As Gwen moved from room to room, adding a throw pillow here, leaning a picture there, her mood lightened. The bones of the house were lovely. The freshly painted walls hid the scars and bruises of the past. It wasn't cheerful, but it had drama. Maybe they could sell this place after all.

"Hello, you here?" Lance's voice rang through the empty rooms.

"In here," Gwen called from the kitchen.

"Hey, our crazed pit bull is looking pretty good this morning."

"Funny."

He dropped three bags onto the counter. "Candles— scented just in case. Crackers—to go with the cheese plates. And toilet paper. We're going to be here all day."

"Good thinking." Gwen opened the package of toilet paper, selected a candle and headed to the guest bathroom off the front hall.

"Have you been upstairs yet?" Lance followed her.

"No. I haven't had a chance."

"I put a few chairs up there, that's it. I didn't want to haul up beds and dressers. But I thought we could add a couple of pillows or throw blankets to warm things up."

"There's a big, plastic garbage bag full of that kind of stuff in the foyer. Help yourself." Gwen busied herself with the toilet paper holder, taking longer than necessary to insert the roll and make a triangular fold in the first sheet.

Lance watched her for a moment then disappeared into the kitchen. She'd go upstairs, just not yet. She'd used up all her courage credits opening the house alone this morning.

Lance had convinced her the figs had attracted the vermin, and although they'd had someone clean up as much of the decaying fruit as possible, the tree was still there. As she lit a candle to leave on the side of the sink, she heard Lance's footsteps on the stairs.

Several minutes later, he joined her in the kitchen. "Can I take those?" He pointed to the last bunch of flowers, bright red gazanias in a milk white jar. "The upstairs hallway needs a little something else."

While Lance finished the second story, Gwen ran to the car for the bag she'd packed with pastries and extra cream and sugar. Wine was fine for the afternoon crowd, but she, for one, wanted to start the day with breakfast.

"Can I help you with that?" Don Gordon pulled up to the curb as Gwen lifted the grocery sack from the trunk. Don, Eric Woo, Carolyn, and Taryn Humboldt—daughter of the founder of Humboldt Realty— climbed out of the vehicle.

"What are you doing here?" Gwen was so surprised to see them, she blurted out the words.

"That's a nice greeting." Don took the bag from Gwen's hand.

"We wanted to see the mystery house," Eric said. "It's the highest-priced listing in the office."

"I brought donuts." Carolyn held up a greasy bag.

The group followed Gwen inside and scattered when they hit the front hall. She could hear the click of heels on the wood floor, creaks overhead, and raised voices from all around the house while she made coffee. She poured the first cup for herself and carried it into the entry-way. "Coffee's ready." From that vantage point, her voice carried into every room.

Don walked down the stairs a moment later and accompanied her to the kitchen. The rest entered through the door off the dining room.

"It's a bit beat up, but it's a great location," Don said.

Lance moved a bite of donut into his cheek. "You should have seen it before we spruced things up."

"The place gives me the creeps," Carolyn said.

Taryn looked at her over the top of her glasses.

Carolyn's hand fluttered in the air as if she was trying to wipe away her words. "I mean, I'm sure it'll sell. The view is amazing. I just wouldn't want to be... "

Taryn put a fist to her mouth and coughed. Carolyn stopped talking.

"I'd better get the signs up." Lance wiped the donut crumbs from his hands onto his pants.

"That's my job," Gwen said.

He rolled his eyes at her and walked out of the kitchen. "Nice guy." Carolyn watched him go with a little too much admiration in her eyes.

"Do you need help with anything?" Taryn said.

"No, I think I'm good." Gwen smiled at her.

Taryn never showed up at her agents' open houses, but then none of her agents had ever had a multimillion-dollar, beachfront listing in Laguna before. Gwen could tell she wanted to stay and make sure she didn't screw things up.

"Let's get going, then," Eric said. "I want to stop by a couple of other places on our way out of town, if that's okay with everybody."

The watchful silence of the house closed around Gwen when the agents left. She felt the raw edge of claustrophobia and hurried to the living room to look out at the ocean. The view from the windows usually had a calming effect on her, but while they'd been in the kitchen drinking coffee and eating donuts, the fog had gotten thicker. The house was now shrouded in gray. The line between sea and sky invisible. She'd heard a storm front was moving in next week.

Gwen shivered.

Carolyn was right. The place was creepy. They could groom it, put a bow on it, but she still didn't trust it. She couldn't get Maricela's words about a house absorbing energy from the deeds committed inside its walls out of her mind.

She wished Lance would get back, but she knew he'd be a while. He had to pound in signs on the highway, north and south, and up and down all the neighboring streets. It was strange how much she'd come to rely on him, even though they'd only been working together a short time. Well, not that surprising really.

Art had always been her rock—solid support, the one she depended on. Not lately. The nasty voice she'd been trying to ignore since she'd seen him and Olivia invaded her head again. *She's younger. She's needy. He won't be able to resist her.* She was tired of quieting that voice, of fighting it.

Gwen let it have full rein. *What if he did leave her for Olivia?*

It would be devastating, but Gwen was about to sell the most expensive property of her career. One listing at this price point would lead to others, too. Real estate was all about groups and communities. Neighbors and buyers with a lot of money to spend would be stopping by today along with the curious and the lookie-loos.

This deal, as difficult and traumatic as it had been, was an incredible opportunity. It meant she wouldn't be dependent on the generosity of her ex-husband like her mother had been. Not that she thought Art was actually going to become an ex-husband, but she was looking at the worst-case scenario, facing her fears.

If Art left her, she'd be okay. She'd found a profession she excelled at, and she'd made a good friend. Her face softened when she thought of Lance. Not romantic thoughts. He probably wasn't interested in her even if she were interested in him. But it was nice to have someone she could rely on.

1.5.4

WHEN LANCE FINALLY RETURNED, he had some of the neighbors in tow—an older couple. They both had short, tousled gray hair and were dressed in running shoes and walking shorts. Gwen watched them as they traversed the foyer, laughing with Lance as if they were old friends.

"We've been wondering what was going on around here," the man said.

"We figured all the banging and buzz saws must mean something good," the wife said.

"There's more that needs doing, but I think we accomplished quite a bit. Come on in." Lance ushered them forward with an extended arm.

"Welcome." Gwen plastered on her best real estate agent smile.

"This is the agent who's managing the property, Gwen Bishop. Gwen, meet Bob and Betty, from three doors down." Lance made introductions.

While Bob and Betty toured the lower story of the house, Gwen and Lance retired to the kitchen. Every new agent learned in Open House 101 that etiquette demanded you allow the potential client to wander through the property alone. You made yourself available to answer questions when and if you were needed.

"I think you're going to be busy." Lance poured himself a cup of coffee. "This house is famous because of the murder. Lots of curious people."

"That's not a good thing," Gwen said.

"Oh, I don't know. They say all publicity is good publicity. Even if people aren't interested in buying this house, they might want to buy another one. Gives you a chance to charm the heck out of them."

Betty-from-three-doors-down popped into the kitchen. "Do you have a flier? My cousin's husband just retired, and they're thinking about moving down to the beach. This place might be too big, but you never know."

Lance handed her paperwork. "Gwen would love to show them what's available in the area." Then he fished a business card from his jeans pocket and dropped his voice to a sexy baritone. "And I'm a general contractor. Tell her not to be afraid of fixers." Betty simpered and took the card.

Gwen observed Lance in action. She came to the conclusion that flirting, for him, was an unconscious act, like a puppy tilting its head and looking adorable when it wanted a treat. Somewhere in his life, he'd learned when he smiled a certain way, talked a certain way, looked at women from the corner of his eye in a certain way, he got what he wanted.

It wouldn't work on her because she understood what he was doing. However, she could see by the expression on Betty's face, it was effective.

Bob stuck his head into the kitchen. "I'm heading upstairs, Betty."

The fascinated expression Betty had been wearing while listening to Lance talk faded. "Coming," she said without so much as a glance toward her husband. "I'll give your card to Stella. I'm sure you'll be hearing from her." With that, she turned and followed her husband from the kitchen.

Gwen shook her head at Lance. "What?" he said.

"You."

"What?" His voice rose a half-octave.

"You know what."

"I don't."

"Drink your coffee," Gwen said.

Footsteps sounded in the foyer. It was Gwen's turn to meet new prospects. She left the kitchen.

This time it was a mother-daughter team. The daughter lived in the area. Mom was visiting and thinking of moving. Based on their awe of the property, Gwen didn't think either woman could come close to affording the home.

However, one never knew. Maricela had sold a Nellie Gail Ranch McMansion to a couple of kids in ripped jeans and t-shirts once. Not everyone who was wealthy flaunted it. She invited the women to look around, and they disappeared down the hall toward the living room.

She was just thinking about heading to the kitchen to refill her coffee cup when a loud cry and a thud echoed through the stairwell. A moment later, Bob-from-three-doors-down appeared on the landing.

"I think you'd better come up here," he said.

Gwen hesitated. She wanted to run for Lance. Send him instead. But she grabbed the newel post and climbed.

Betty leaned against the wall outside the master bedroom, a hand covering her mouth. Bob stood back to let Gwen walk by. Neither spoke.

Gwen looked at her feet. They were clad in the expensive pumps she'd gotten on sale at Nordstrom's. They looked confident. They took one bold step after another. She tried not to think about where they were taking her, or what she'd see when she got there. She just focused on her self-assured shoes. When her feet reached the end of the hall, Gwen forced her eyes to enter the bedroom.

At first, she didn't understand what she was looking at. She saw only colors—white and red—no distinct shapes. It was modern art. Something that gave the effect of a thing without being that thing.

The interpretation came to her all at once, like one of those pictures you have to stare at for several minutes before you can see the dragon hidden in it. It was an impressionistic tableau depicting the death of Sondra Olsen. The last thing Gwen saw before a wash of black covered her vision was milk white fur splashed with scarlet in a heap on the rug covering dark hardwood.

Gwen lay on the floor in one of the small bedrooms atop a throw blanket she'd brought from home. A pillow was under her head. Betty-from-three-doors-down sat next to her, a glass of wine clutched in her hand.

"Want some?" she said, lifting her glass a couple of inches.

Gwen eased herself onto her elbows. "Where's Lance?"

"He's..." she paused. "Cleaning things up."

A wave of nausea pushed Gwen back.

"Who would do a thing like that?" Betty said.

Who would do a thing like that? A rhetorical question. No real answer, so Gwen didn't say anything.

"The poor opossum. They're not my favorite creatures, but I am an animal lover. I have a Pekingese. But, really, who would do that to a defenseless creature? It's unconscionable," Betty said.

Unconscionable, good word. The kind of person who would kill an opossum and leave its body on display exactly where Sondra Olsen was found had to be without conscience.

"Someone must not want this house sold, that's all I can think. But such a cruel prank. There must be other ways to stop the sale of a house." Betty gulped her wine.

Something switched on in Gwen's frazzled brain. She'd considered it before but disregarded it. However, she now realized the simplest explanation was probably the correct one—Occam's Razor. Someone didn't want the house sold; ergo, that someone had planted the roaches and the rat to scare her off. When that didn't work, they resorted to killing Sondra Olsen again in effigy.

"This house used to be such a nice place." Betty was still talking. "Lilly was a lovely person. When she was alive, the front yard was immaculate. I was only inside once or twice, but the decor was stunning. She'd done it all herself. I thought she'd used a professional decorator, but she said no."

Gwen's mind was spinning. *Who had access to the house?* Besides her, Lance, and... *Could there be an insurance policy that would yield more money for Fiona than a sale? Could she be building a saboteur scenario because she was planning to burn the place down?*

Gwen rejected that idea almost at once. This property commanded a huge price tag in the current market. Insurance companies would use comparable sales. Nothing had sold in this neighborhood for at least a year, giving an adjuster an excuse to lower the payout. Besides, why would Fiona hire her, sabotage the sale, then commit arson? A sale was a clean, legitimate, safe path to income.

"When Lilly died, Edward let the place go. He was bereft, the poor man. Almost a hermit. I think the only person he saw regularly was his daughter—the dancer. She would come by on Sundays. It was a shame." Betty prattled on, but Gwen no longer listened.

She'd put an official Board of Realty lockbox on the house two days ago. Every agent in the office had access to the code. Another agent was the only kind of person she could think of who might want her to lose the listing. An agent who wanted it for him or herself. Gwen had met some competitive realtors in her time, some who would sink pretty low to get a good listing, but killing an opossum and leaving its bloodied corpse in the master bedroom? It beleaguered the imagination.

"When Edward couldn't manage alone anymore, his daughter put him in a nursing home in San Juan. I don't know what was wrong with him. Hazel, next door—" Betty pointed right. "Thought he had Alzheimer's. Anyway, the place fell into disrepair after he left."

"Maybe I should have some wine." Gwen didn't really want a drink, only a moment to think in peace.

"Certainly, dear." Betty patted her arm and left the room.

1.5.5

GWEN STARED at the ceiling and began to sort through possible suspects. Taryn didn't work with clients anymore and stood to gain when the property sold anyway. She was out.

Carolyn was ambitious, but too flighty to carry off the kind of complex campaign that had been waged. Besides, Carolyn was a soft touch for animals. She'd wouldn't kill a rat, never mind an opossum.

One by one, Gwen evaluated all the agents in the office and dismissed them, until she got to Don Gordon. He'd come to mind first, but she'd wanted to be fair, to analyze the others before blaming him. However, he was competitive, mean-spirited, and he was a man.

The attacks seemed masculine in nature. Women generally didn't like to get their hands dirty. A woman would be more inclined to use slander, innuendo, or psychological assaults than dead animals. At least, the women in her office would.

The more she thought about it, the more pieces of the puzzle fell into place. She sat up. She was sure. Don Gordon must be the culprit.

Fury revived her. She pushed herself off the floor and came to her feet in one motion. She needed to talk to Lance. If Don thought he could intimidate her, get her to walk away from the listing, he was wrong. Dead wrong.

She traversed the hallway in long strides, her aversion to the master bedroom washed away in a flood of outrage. She found Lance squatting next to a bucket full of pink, sudsy water, scrubbing the wood floor with a large sponge. He looked at her as she entered, concern etched into the lines of his face.

"I know who did this," she said.

Lance rocked back on his heels. "You look like you're feeling better."

"Don Gordon."

Lance's eyebrows rose. "That agent who was here earlier?"

"Yes, him. This... this person," Gwen waved a hand at the floor, "must have been trying to stop the sale of the house. What other motive could they have?"

"You think Don wants a top salesman plaque so badly he'd resort to this?" Lance's voice was skeptical.

"No. I think he wants the listing. Money is a big motivator."

"He might want the listing, but even if you lost it, or walked away from it, what's to say he'd get it?"

"If he's the one sabotaging me, he knows what's happening behind the scenes. I tell Maricela everything, and his desk is only a few yards away." A surge of anger coursed through Gwen like caffeine. She marched to the far wall and back. "Fiona told me another agent from the office pitched her. What do you want to bet it was him?"

Lance dropped the sponge into the bucket and stood. "It seems like a stretch."

Gwen threw up her hands. "Who else, then? Who else could possibly have done this?"

"I don't know, Gwen, but it's not our job to figure it out." Lance's voice was annoyingly soothing.

"You're not talking about getting the police involved?"

"I don't think we have a choice. Sondra Olsen's murderer might have been the one who did this."

"Sondra's murderer is long gone. He moved on to Newport Beach." Gwen stopped pacing and faced him. "I know I've been terrified he'd show up again, but I was wrong. You were right."

"About what?"

"A cockroach infestation doesn't sound like the work of a homicidal maniac. These crimes, or pranks, whatever you want to call them, were done by someone else. I'm telling you, it's Don. The last thing this place needs is more bad press. If we call the police, we'll be playing right into his hands."

"You think the murders were coincidental?"

Gwen ran a hand through her hair. She was still processing her thoughts. "Not coincidental, but they gave the prankster ideas. I think there are two separate perpetrators."

Lance looked skeptical. "A murderer and a prankster?"

"Right. You always thought the roaches and the rat were innocent, that they happened because of the figs."

He gave her an almost imperceptible nod.

"We now know they weren't, but it doesn't mean they have anything to do with the murders."

"The opossum was arranged like—"

Gwen cut him off. She didn't want to think about the opossum. "There were pictures and descriptions of the murder scene all over the internet."

"True," he said.

"Think this through with me." She held up a hand and ticked off her arguments on her fingers. "Don has information the general public isn't privy to. He has motive and opportunity. He was here this morning, wandering around the house by himself."

"How did he get the opossum into the house without our seeing him?"

"I changed the lockbox on Thursday night. He could have planted it in the closet, then pulled it out this morning when no one was around."

"Can't you check with the security company and see if he's used his key since the box has been on?"

"I'll do it on Monday, but meanwhile, let's not call the police. At least, not yet."

"All right. I don't think the cops would be very interested, anyway." Lance inhaled and exhaled slowly. "But as far as motive goes, I still say it's a crapshoot whether Don would get the listing or not, even if you did give it up. I mean, Fiona could decide to pull the house off the market, or sign with someone else. Anything could happen."

"True. But Don is so competitive I think he'd be happy just to take the listing away from me. It's a no-lose situation for him."

Lance picked up the bucket. "Supposing you're right. It's Don. What's the plan? We can't confront him. We have no proof."

Gwen followed him into the hallway and down the stairs. "Well, for one thing, we don't cancel the open house."

"The only sign I took down was the one out front. I could put it up again."

"We don't tell anyone. We act like nothing happened."

"That would piss him off." She could hear the smile in Lance's voice. "What do we do about Bob and Betty?"

"Let me handle them," Gwen said.

Lance headed outside to clean the bucket, and Gwen went in search of the neighbors. She found them in the dining room. Bob sat in a chair and Betty stood, a wine glass in each of her hands. "You must be feeling better," she said when she saw Gwen.

"I am, thanks." Gwen took one of the glasses from her. "Can we talk?"

Betty sat across from her husband and folded her hands on the table like a schoolgirl waiting for instruction.

"I'm so sorry you were exposed to this. I feel responsible." Gwen held up a hand when they began to protest.

"How could you be responsible?" Bob said. "This was obviously the work of a reprehensible deviant. The price of the homes may make this neighborhood exclusive to live in, but you don't have to present a credit statement to visit. There is constant coming and going of all sorts, scuba divers in the mornings, beach bums and tourists all afternoon. I have to tell you; I've been thinking about selling. Moving to a gated community."

A small smile tickled at the corner of Gwen's mouth. It would be a wonderful irony if all of Don's efforts to steal this listing from her resulted in her acquiring another one. "If you're thinking about selling, you'll understand when I ask you to please keep what happened here today quiet. For Fiona's sake."

"Fiona?" Bob repeated the name.

"Ed's daughter," Betty said. "I assume she owns the property now."

"Yes," Gwen said. "She was very shaken by the death that occurred in the house. She might be afraid this incident was directed at her in some way. I don't think it was. I think your assessment of the situation is the correct one. It was a random act by a transient, or some kid taking a dare. But it might be hard to convince her of that."

"I'd hate to upset her, but... " Betty let her words trail off.

"Plus, you know how people are," Gwen said. "If word got around about this, it could affect the sale of the house. Actually, it could affect values in the whole neighborhood, your house even. Nobody wants to spend several million on a home and then have to worry about vandals."

Bob and Betty looked across the table at each other, communicating without words the way people who've been married for many years do. The way Gwen and Art had done until recently. Seeming to come to an agreement, they rose as one.

"I believe you're right," Bob said. "It's not like there's a crime wave on Cliff Drive. No need to involve the police, or the gossips."

"Exactly," Gwen said, walking them toward the door. "You have my card? I'd love to help you if you decide to relocate."

By the time Bob-and-Betty-from-three-doors-down left the premises, Gwen had them securely in her camp.

1.5.6

WHEN THE FINAL STRAGGLERS LEFT, Gwen shut the door behind them and kicked off her pumps. Despite the horrible start to the day, the open house had gone well. One couple had seemed very interested in the house, and she'd handed out at least ten business cards.

Gwen wandered to the deck and sat on one of the camp chairs Lance had moved outside. He'd left ten minutes earlier to pull the signs. It was nice to have a moment alone. She lifted a foot onto the opposite knee and massaged it. Standing in heels all day was murder.

The sun was setting, the colors creating a romantic, fairy tale sky. Deep magenta clouds bloomed above a midnight blue sea. They were the same color as the roses Gwen had placed in the living room.

Her cell phone rang from inside the house. The foxhunt ringtone meant it was Art. She sighed, pushed herself out of the chair, and padded inside to answer it.

"Hi, honey. How'd the open house go?" Art's voice was warm.

"Fine. How're the kids?" Hers was cool. They needed to have a conversation about the alley, soon. But not on the phone. Not now.

"Fine. I took them to In-N-Out, so they're happy." Gwen felt a momentary twinge of annoyance. Art hadn't bothered asking what she was doing for dinner. "What time are you home?" he asked.

"Not sure." She didn't elaborate.

"I was thinking about going out for a bit."

"Where?" Her question held a sharp note. She cleared her throat.

"The hospital," he said.

Gwen didn't speak for a long moment, then said, "Why?"

"Brian's awake and lucid. I'd like to talk to him."

"Why?" she asked again.

There were several beats of silence before he spoke. When he did, he didn't answer her question. "Gwen, what's wrong?"

"What do you mean, what's wrong?"

"You're mad at me. I can hear it in your voice."

"I'm not mad," she lied. "It's just, you're on kid duty."

"I've been with them all day." Now Art sounded irritated. "Jason can take over for a couple of hours."

"Will she be there?" The question popped out before Gwen had time to think about it. She wished she could take it back.

"She?"

"Oh, come on."

"Olivia?"

"Of course, *Olivia*." Gwen accentuated her name.

"She's his mother."

"In other words, yes. She'll be there."

Another long pause, then, "Yes. Is that a problem?"

It was, but how could she explain without telling him she'd been hiding in the alley? She wished with every fiber of her being that she'd confronted them that day, but she hadn't. If she said something now, it would look like she was the guilty party, and she wasn't. "You spend a lot of time with her," she said instead.

"I'm not going to apologize for that, Gwen. I feel it's the right thing to do." Now, he sounded militant.

"Hello." Lance's voice rang from the foyer.

"In here," Gwen called back.

"Can we talk about this tonight? When I get home?" Art said.

She heard Lance banging around in the kitchen. "Sure."

"I'll see you later." Art's voice went deep and throaty. "Love you, babe." And the line went dead. The room felt hollow.

Love you, babe.

Did he?

She heard a rumble of thunder. It had been threatening rain all week. As Gwen returned her phone to her purse, her arm brushed the roses sitting on the narrow table by the window, releasing their scent. It smelled like a funeral. She normally loved roses. It was this house. It had a way of ruining everything. She moved away.

As the first fat drops hit the window, Lance entered the living room. "I found some wine in a bag in the cupboard. Hope you don't mind I opened a bottle." He handed her a glass of red wine.

She didn't mind, not at all. "You found my stash of Red Ravish."

His eyes widened over the rim of his glass. "Tastes expensive."

"It's one of my favorites."

He looked stricken. "I'm sorry. I assumed they were extra bottles meant for the open house."

"I brought it for us," she said. "So we could celebrate." This wasn't entirely true. The truth was, she'd bought the bottles on Friday, meant to bring them home, but inadvertently left them in the car. When she saw them there that morning, she thought she should bring them inside in case the weather got warm and the wine was ruined by the heat.

"That was very nice of you." He lifted his glass in a toast.

Lightning flashed across the sky as she returned the gesture. Lance set his glass down and bolted out to the patio. He returned a moment later with the camp chairs. "Only a little damp." He wiped one of the chairs with his sleeve and gestured for her to sit. She did, and he pulled up the other chair next to her.

"Remember the man with the baseball cap?" he asked.

"Which one?" Gwen laughed.

"The Angel's cap. I asked him about it."

"Oh, yeah."

"He wants me to stop by and give him a bid on a kitchen remodel."

"Great."

"And I think that Goth-looking couple from LA were really interested in this place."

"I do, too."

The warmth of the wine worked its way through Gwen's system and she began to relax for the first time that day. It was nice. Sitting and sipping and watching the storm together. She felt a sense of camaraderie she hadn't felt in a long time.

Lance laughed at her jokes and finished her sentences. She knew what he was going to say about the people who'd gone through the house before he said it.

After a bit, Gwen stared into her empty glass. "I need more wine."

"I'll get it."

Lance started to rise, but she put a hand on his arm. "Let me."

She found the open bottle in the kitchen next to the remnants of the snacks she'd laid out earlier. She piled the leftover cheese from three almost empty platters onto one, added two bunches of grapes—all that was left from the fruit tray— and arranged the last of a box of crackers around the edge. Then, she grabbed the bottle of wine and carried both into the living room.

"Dinner." She set the platter on the table, shoving the roses to one side. They refilled their glasses and settled in to watch the storm again. A half hour later, they'd opened the second bottle of wine.

"If Bob-and-Betty-from-three-doors-down decide to sell, you'll get the listing," Lance announced.

"Why do you say that?" Gwen asked.

"Bob couldn't keep his eyes off you."

Gwen's cheeks flushed, but it wasn't an unpleasant feeling.

"Well, Betty had the hots for you."

Lance groaned. "Not my type."

"And you think Bob is mine?"

"No, no, I didn't say that," he said with a laugh. "I only said, you're his."

Gwen lifted her glass to hide her smile. She took a long sip of wine. "I guess it's nice to know someone admires you, even if it isn't someone, you know..." She wasn't sure how to finish the sentence.

"Someone you wish admired you?" Lance said.

"Right."

Their easy banter dried up, and neither spoke for a long minute. The rain beating against the window filled the silence. Finally, Lance said, "Who do you wish admired you, Gwen?"

She stiffened. "My husband."

She'd intended the words to derail the awkward turn the conversation had taken, but they only seemed to make things worse.

"Doesn't he?" Lance turned meltingly warm eyes on her.

Maricela was right. He was too handsome. Gwen looked away. "That's not what I meant."

"What did you mean?"

She opened her mouth to say something witty, or cutting, or just plain silly, but found herself telling Lance all about the alley.

1.5.7

THE BOTTLE WAS EMPTY. Gwen upended it over her glass, but nothing came out. Which was probably for the best. She'd had too much already.

"Sometimes you don't appreciate what you've got until you try something else," Lance said.

Gwen stared at him, her pulse quickening just a little. "What are you talking about?"

He got up quickly, disappeared, then reappeared holding a full bottle of wine. "I snuck one into the pantry when you switched from coffee and sweets to wine and cheese." He topped off both their glasses. "It's not Red Ravish, but..."

Gwen felt a mix of emotions—embarrassment, relief, and something else. Something she didn't want to put a name to. She sipped, then rested the hand that held the glass on the arm of her chair. "Thanks for listening."

"You know, you may disagree with me, but I don't believe people are naturally monogamous."

"Oh, that's comforting." Her tone was sarcastic.

"I don't mean you and Art. I'm talking, generally speaking." He waved his wine glass. "Just look at the culture. Half of marriages end in divorce, right?"

"So marriage is a farce? That's what you're saying?" The warmth of the evening was dissipating into the chilly night air.

"No, no, not at all. I'm saying maybe the institution of marriage should be a little more flexible." He stroked her hand that rested on the arm of her chair. "If people bent with their biology, relationships might not break so often."

Gwen pulled her hand out from under his. "My father bent with his biology. He screwed around on my mother, then left her for a younger woman."

"I'm not advocating that." Lance's voice was soothing. "People who want to have an external relationship need to pick the right kind of person."

"There's a right kind of person to have an affair with?"

He stared into his wine glass. "It has to be someone who has the same goals for the relationship. Someone who's okay with not being first in their life. Someone who respects their marriage."

"That makes no sense. If I respect marriage, the last thing I'm going to do is have an affair with a married man—or an unmarried one, for that matter." The conversation was making Gwen uncomfortable again. She took a gulp of wine.

"What if, hypothetically, marriages were better off, lasted longer, and were happier when they had outside help?"

Was he serious? He was pulling her leg, surely. She studied his face.

It was a stunning face, perfect for the cover of a romance novel. Large, dreamy, espresso-brown eyes sat above high cheekbones. His gold-brown hair was tousled. It begged to have fingers run through it.

She stood abruptly. "I've got to go." She'd stood too quickly. The room began to spin around her.

"Hey, hey." Lance got up, put his hands on her shoulders and steadied her. "You okay?"

His lips were inches away from hers. She'd never noticed how full they were. A second later, she was kissing them. Two seconds later, she broke away, horrified at what she'd done.

Lance held onto one of her hands. "I'd never try to come between you and Art. You have a family to think about." He picked up her hand, turned it palm up, and kissed it.

A nest of butterflies stirred to life in her stomach. Want and need batted their wings against her rib cage. Her heart thudded. "I... I can't."

He dropped her hand. "You can't drive, either." He sat and patted her chair. "Better sit."

He was right. She was too far gone to drive. She sat.

"Did you see the master bathroom?" he asked.

The change in conversation was so abrupt, it startled her.

"No. I never made it in there."

"I think it's some of my best work."

"Oh?" Where was he going with this?

"We should christen it."

The thudding of her heart returned. A vision of sitting in that bath with Lance, candles glowing around them, burst into her mind unbidden. A coal of heat lit her belly.

He turned to look at her, a mischievous grin on his face. "Really. Let's take a bath."

"Lance." She gave a quick shake of her head as if to rid it of the earlier image.

"We don't have to do anything you don't want to do." He picked up her hand again and played with her fingers. "Just relax together."

She didn't speak. Couldn't speak.

"We deserve it." He stood, suddenly all business. "Besides, you need to sober up. It'll kill some time."

Gwen found her voice. "I have to straighten up the kitchen."

"Don't be long." And with that, he left the living room.

A few minutes later, Gwen heard water running and Lance moving around upstairs. She pushed out of the deck chair, waited a moment for the room to settle, and made her way into the kitchen.

She cleaned up the platters and plates with mechanical movements, her mind on what was happening upstairs. *Was she really going up there?*

He'd said they wouldn't do anything she didn't want to do. The problem was, a part of her wanted to do things she knew she shouldn't.

"Ha," she said aloud.

Who was she kidding? She shouldn't go upstairs at all, shouldn't get naked, shouldn't climb into a tub with another man. It didn't matter if they did anything else. That was enough. She'd felt betrayed just seeing Art hugging another woman, and they were fully clothed.

Her phone dinged with a text from Lance.

> Coming?

She dried her hands on a towel.

> Yes, almost done

> Hurry.

And a smile emoji.

A smile emoji? Really?

"This is crazy," Gwen said to her reflection in the darkened kitchen window.

> Yes.

She was hurrying, but she couldn't understand why. Even in her alcohol muddled brain, she knew she wasn't going to go through with it. The part of her that wanted to go upstairs was weakening, and the part of her that knew she should walk out the front door was growing stronger.

> I brought more wine up. I'll drink it all.

Gwen sighed.

> You do that.

> Don't make me drink alone.

This didn't sound like the man who'd just told her the bath was to sober her up. She put the last of the dishes into a bag to bring to the car and wiped down the counters with a sponge.

The phone pinged.

Waiting.

"I know," she answered out loud while she typed the words. She had lost her mind for one minute, but she'd found it again. She'd leave. Go home to her husband. Tell him about the alley. Work it out.

She crossed the living room, extinguishing candles as she went. The dread and fear this house often filled her with returned as darkness replaced the light. When she reached the fireplace, she turned off the gas and was momentarily blinded by the echo of the flames. A streak of lightning pointed like a finger across the black room to the foyer; thunder rolled.

She moved in that direction and stood at the base of the stairs looking into the dark cavern at the top. Love you, babe. Art's words rang through her mind. A primal yearning for Lance hit her, but she couldn't go through with this. Wouldn't. Maybe she was a fool. Maybe Art had cheated on her. Maybe he hadn't. Either way, nothing would make this right.

She'd lived her whole adult life mourning her mother's death. A death caused by her father's affair. Gwen didn't believe in bending biology, or flexible marriages. It didn't matter how handsome, or dependable, or persuasive Lance was. She knew the reality of infidelity.

She didn't want to leave him in the tub wondering where she was, though. That didn't seem right. She'd climb the stairs, go into the bathroom, and tell him she couldn't do it. If it cost her a friendship, so be it. Several shots of adrenaline hit her blood stream like espresso at the thought, but she began to climb.

The feeling that something was wrong hit her on the third riser. There was no warning creak like in a haunted house movie. Everything was quiet. Too quiet.

She heard no splashing, no running water, no sound at all other than the murmur of rain against the windowpanes. When she reached the top of the stairs, she called out to Lance.

He didn't answer.

She paused for a moment, then fixated on the trail of moonlight coming from the open door at the end of the hall. The bright path led her down the dark corridor and into the master suite.

From halfway across the bedroom, she could see the tile floor of the bathroom shining wetly in the candlelight. Lance must have splashed water out of the tub as he got into it. With a soft, nervous laugh she said, "We're going to have to mop."

Lance didn't answer.

A strand of hair tickled her shoulder. She slapped it behind her as if she could slap away the light fingers of anxiety tickling up and down her spine. She stepped over the puddle into the master bath.

Her eyes followed the droplets to the wide, ceramic tub. Rose petals floated on the surface of the water like drops of blood. Lance's chin rested on his chest as if he were sleeping. "Lance." Her voice broke like a teenage boy's. She cleared her throat and stepped closer.

His knees rose like bone, white islands. She noticed, in an absent-minded way, his legs were skinnier than she'd imagined them. Burgundy clouds floated in the sudsy water.

"Lance." Her voice was pleading now.

She willed him to open his eyes, to smile sheepishly and tell her he'd spilled a glass of wine into the tub. But he didn't stir. Only his fine, brown, chest hairs swayed in the water like kelp.

DING. The light of her cell phone shone blue and ghostly in the dim room.

Finally. You're here.

The phone slipped from her fingers and disappeared beneath the maroon bubbles.

1.5.8

THERE WAS something hypnotic about Lance's fingers bobbing white and lifeless in the scarlet water. Gwen stared stupidly, until a current of thoughts washed over her like ice water. Someone had killed him. They'd hidden somewhere in the house. They'd waited until he was naked and vulnerable. They'd slit his throat.

She pressed her hand to her mouth to stifle a scream. *Get away.* She had to leave. Now.

She stepped backward, distancing herself from the gruesome sight, then stumbled under the force of another wave of impressions.

The texts.

Who had sent them? Not Lance. Was that person still here? In the house? She spun toward the bedroom.

The only illumination came from watery moonlight shining through the uncovered windows. Her eyes ran across the expanse of dark floor to the doorway leading into the hall. Dark, indistinct mounds loomed between her and the exit. She stepped forward, wary and alert— a deer sidling toward a salt lick.

A shape on the bed rippled in the blackness. Gwen stared. Was it a trick of moonlight? She strained her ears for a rustle of bed sheets, but all she heard was the pounding of her pulse.

Lightning flashed. In that split second, Gwen saw an arm cradling a head. Another flash. She saw feet crossed in a relaxed, picnic-in-the-park pose.

"I've been enjoying the wine. It's nowhere near as good as your favorite red, but it's definitely passable for an inexpensive blend," a deep voice said. The shape rose onto an elbow. A shadowed arm hoisted a toast.

Incredulity almost extinguished Gwen's fear. The voice was familiar. The man put his glass on the bedside table and turned on a low lamp. She knew him—knew, but couldn't comprehend. It was absurd. It was as if a Martian, or Abraham Lincoln, or the Ghost of Christmas Past were lying in that bed.

His eyes gleamed, feral in the low light. How had she not noticed those eyes before? He patted the bed. "You look as ravishing as your favorite wine. Come, sit. Let's talk."

"What are you doing here?" As soon as she asked the question, she wished she wouldn't have. Its answer lurked in the shadows of the empty house.

"We have things to discuss."

It must be shock or the alcohol still coursing through her blood-stream. She couldn't fit the pieces together. The events of the day swam in meaningless circles through the squall in her mind. He was here. In Fiona's home. And must have been all evening, while she and Lance...

Lance, oh god, Lance.

The fact that he was lying dead in the bath burst through the unre-ality of the scene and struck her like another cold wave. She began to shiver.

Mo sat up. He swung his legs over the side of the bed. Heartbeats scampered around her chest, but she was unable to move. Like a mouse mesmerized by a cobra, she watched as he crossed the room. He stood between her and the door to the hall, between her and her family.

A primal instinct took hold of her unresponsive limbs. She broke into a run and launched herself at him. It was like slamming into Mount Vesuvius. She fell back, stunned.

"No need to be hasty. I was coming to you." He grinned.

Gwen dodged right; he blocked her. She feinted left. He spread his arms wide and sidestepped.

"Calm down. I told you, I only want to talk," he said.

Gwen tasted the sour bile of panic. She opened her mouth to reason with him, plead if she had to, but all that came was a guttural moan. She retreated. He followed.

"You're a strong woman, a woman who gets what she wants. I've been watching you," he said.

Gwen stepped farther away. She inhaled and exhaled slowly, willing herself to control the fear crawling over her skin. If she could humor him, distract him, maybe she could reach the wall switch by the closet behind her. It controlled the bedside table lamp he'd turned on. She had no further plan, just hide in the dark, away from those feral eyes.

"I don't know what you're talking about," Gwen said.

"Oh, you know. You were going to..." He spread his hands, jerked his head toward the bed and raised his eyebrows.

"It wasn't... " Her words trailed off. She wouldn't defend herself. Not to this man. She had to focus on the light switch. That small piece of plastic became her talisman. It was the only thing standing between her and complete panic, and the only thing in the world that mattered at this moment was diverting his attention away from it. "What do you want?"

"Not as much as Lance did, I can assure you. I have a simple favor to ask."

"Favor? You killed Lance because you want a favor?" A hysterical laugh burbled from Gwen's lips. She bit it off. "What kind of favor could you possibly want from me?"

"A small one."

She swallowed the terror rising in her throat and forced herself to calm. Predators reacted to fear. Fear would make her prey. Be angry, Gwen. Turn the fear into anger.

"Why should I help you? What's in it for me?" She narrowed her eyes and feigned suspicious interest.

Mo's fingers twitched. He grabbed the leg of his pants, and they stilled. "For starters, I won't blow the whistle on you and your boyfriend. The police will think you killed poor Lance if I leave him there, you know. Not to mention how hubby would feel about it if he knew what you were up to. I will swear you were in The Leaky Barrel with me all evening. Wine tasting."

The switch was only feet away now, but he stood too close for her to reach it unnoticed.

"And, of course, there's your life. Help me, or—" He shrugged and lifted his palms to the ceiling.

Gwen jumped at the implication, and her back slammed into the wall. Something hard and small jutted into her hip. "What do I need to do?" Her words came in panted breaths.

"Just make sure this property doesn't sell to anyone but me."

Her fingers walked up the wall toward her low back. "That's it?"

"Maybe one or two other little things." He waved a dismissive hand.

Gwen felt along the plastic ridge of the switch with imperceptible movements. She relaxed her facial muscles into an expression of resignation. "I guess I don't have much choice, do I?"

"I believe I have you over the proverbial barrel." He chuckled at his own joke.

She flipped the switch. Blackness fell. She slipped toward the bed. His arms knocked against the wall where she'd stood a half-second before.

"Oh, very clever," he said into the darkness. "How will I find you with the lights out?"

She found the lamp in the dark, yanked it from the wall and climbed onto the bed. She heard the light switch click uselessly.

Everything was still for a moment, then the noise of his breath, the sour wine smell of him, the shuffle of his feet moved closer. Brandishing the lamp in her right hand, she used her left to guide her. She crept across the width of the California King mattress.

"Have you ever played searchlight?" he said.

Gwen didn't answer. She heard the smack of flesh on wood. Mo cursed.

A minute passed. He said, "I used to watch children playing on the beach at night. They used flashlights to tag and capture each other. I should have brought one." He sniffed the air like a hunting dog.

Gwen felt the mattress sag under the pressure of his hand. She slid off the far end of the bed and dropped to her knees.

Lightning lit the room, then thunder rumbled. She huddled into a small ball and hugged the edge of the bed.

"Where are you, little Gwen?" Frustration laced his voice.

Gwen, eyes now adjusted to the moonlight, could see the bedroom doorway only yards away. It might as well be a mile. If she could see shapes in the shadows, so could he. She felt the bed heave and heard his steps—more confident this time— coming toward her.

"Come out, come out wherever you are," he said in a sing-song.

Gwen gripped the lamp and drew her feet underneath herself.

"I'm tired of this game." He sounded peevish.

She readied herself to spring and swing at him. He rounded the bed. A wet sheen on his forehead glistened in the gloom.

They made eye contact.

Before Gwen could react, she saw a quick movement in her peripheral vision. Pain reverberated through her skull, then nothing.

MOLLY: Sorry, people, I hate to leave you here, but we are out of time.

The question I'm posing to you this episode is this: Did you guess Mo was our killer? Did you have any idea our mild-mannered wine merchant was, in fact, REK? Let me know, but be honest. I truly wouldn't have known if I hadn't read the court transcripts.

Join me next time for more *Murders Under the Sun.*

(cue music)

VO: If you enjoyed this episode, please leave us a five-star review on your favorite podcast service—it really helps. *Murders Under the Sun* is edited by Jim Wilbourne, theme music is by Eclectic Blends, and I'm your host, Molly Shure.

part seven

MURDERS UNDER THE SUN
SEASON ONE; EPISODE SIX

MOLLY: Welcome back to *Murders Under the Sun*. I'm Molly Shure, your host.

After the last episode, where we left Gwen in a dark, empty house with the Real Estate Killer, tons of you emailed and railed on me on social media. I get it, you were angry about the cliff hanger—no pun intended.

Honestly, as you'll hear today, there wasn't a good place to stop the narrative. The rest of the story moves as fast as a bullet train. And my producers want me to keep these episodes under two hours. So, my apologies, but I'm not sure what else I could've done.

Today, you'll hear from REK—or Mo, as we now know—a couple of times. But honestly, the most harrowing parts of the story are from Gwen's perspective. After the interview, she told me that this experience changed her forever.

I didn't know her before, but I can tell you she is a very strong woman today. What doesn't kill you makes you stronger, right? But enough philosophizing. I've made you wait long enough. Here's Mo.

1.6.2

THE DAY STARTED UNBELIEVABLY WELL. I saw Gwen's car coming up Cliff Drive from a window in one of the front bedrooms. I watched as she pulled up to the curb and carried several parcels into the house.

When I heard the click of her heels on the floor downstairs, I left the front bedroom, hurried down the hall in my stocking feet, and positioned myself in the walk-in closet of the master bedroom. I waited.

Before I had time to set up my surprise for Gwen, several people came into the room at once. I was so startled, I bumped into a shelf, and something thudded to the floor. I feared I'd given myself away, but there was an auspicious cough from the other side of the closet door at the same moment. It must have covered the noise. No one came to investigate. When they left, I sneaked out, staged the room, then returned to my hole.

The opossum had the exact effect I'd hoped. Better actually. Before I gloat, however, let me set the record straight. I didn't kill the thing. I'm not a monster. I'd found it by the side of the road, hit by a car. It had given me ideas.

I'd left the closet door open a crack to watch the action, and almost laughed aloud when Gwen fell into a dead faint. I hadn't expected that. There were cracks in her armor after all.

Sure I wouldn't have long to wait before the open house shut down and I could emerge from my cramped hideout, I hid behind a built-in chest of drawers where I could still see through the open door. Several times, I leaned against the wall and dozed. Imagine my chagrin when the event proceeded as if nothing had happened. All day long, I heard the movements and voices of people coming and going.

Once or twice, I almost crept out just to see what was happening, but I'm glad I refrained. Good things come to those who wait. Waiting revealed Gwen's Achilles' heel.

The scent of roses was the first clue that a splendid opportunity was about to present itself. The second, the view of Lance filling the bathtub and dropping rose petals into the water. Romance was in the air.

Catching the gigolo with his pants down was almost too good to be true. He was easy to deal with, half-drunk, eyes closed, and naked as a jaybird. His death was as smooth as a good Cabernet.

Gwen was more difficult. I hadn't expected her to turn out the lights and bolt, but even that was only a momentary setback. Thankfully, I'd brought my old nightstick along. I'd liberated it from one of my mother's boyfriends when I was a boy. It had been a favorite toy.

I enjoyed the chase. It reinforced my original notion that she might come in handy. Gwen had grit and ingenuity. Yet, based on her fling with Lance, she seemed willing to break a few rules. And I now had something to hold over her head. The last thing she'd want would be for her religious husband to find out what she'd been up to.

I hated to leave her with my treasure in the basement, but I couldn't think of anywhere else on such short notice. I'll only keep her there until it's safe to move her. My apartment will draw less attention than the last place she's been seen.

I'd like to release her. How else is she going to work for me? That's impossible, however, until I'm sure she fully embraces the consequences of not going along with my plans. The consequences are, of course, inevitable. However, hope makes fools of us all. She will do what I say in order to stay alive, even if she knows in her heart of hearts what the final outcome will be. People always do.

Disposing of Lance's body was more difficult than killing him. It wouldn't do to let the police find him here. I've been down that road before, and I need everyone to believe that the lovers ran off together.

I waited until the street was quiet, carried his body to the side yard and began to dig. I buried him between the fig tree and the bushes. The dirt had already been disturbed, thanks to the landscape work that had been started, but it was still time consuming. I was sweating and filthy by the time I was done.

After cleaning myself up, I got rid of Gwen's car. I drove the vehicle to Long Beach, parked near the airport, and walked several blocks to an all-night bar. There I had a glass of abysmal wine to calm my nerves, then called an Uber. It will be a few days before the vehicle is found, I imagine. By then, Gwen will either be my real estate agent or she'll be dead.

When I finally returned to my shop, I was so agitated I paced between the shelves for over an hour, running a finger across the bottles —my form of meditation. It calmed me, helped me think. I drew on the strength of the wine.

Every bottle represents an ancient process, a magic formula. Every crop of grapes demands its own unique care. Was it a hot, dry year? Wet and cold? An early or late spring? Nature infuses the grape with a mystery only the alchemist can unravel.

He combines varietals—dark with bright, sweet with pungent— to achieve balance. He adds a pinch of this, a drop of that, then hides his creation away in the dark. The longer it sits, the more deep and complex it becomes. Every wine has its perfect time. Opened too soon, it will be weak and shallow. Too late, and it's spoiled.

This was my time. My sister wouldn't win. She wouldn't steal my birthright.

One night about a year ago, I sat in my car across the street from her home. From my dark, solitary perch, I could see her through the windows of that bright, open space. I watched her the way I had when she was a girl.

It came to me then. Literally. It came to me. I wasn't looking for a counter-spell, an antidote. I didn't believe there was one.

It was getting late. She was sitting at her kitchen table reading. I hadn't seen her husband through the windows in a while. I assumed he'd gone to bed. I was tired and thinking about doing the same when she stood.

She walked to the doorway of the kitchen. The room went black. In a second, she reappeared in the dining room, crossed it, and disappeared into black again. The vision repeated in the office. Then the living room. I watched her disappear again and again.

When the last light was extinguished, my mind was illuminated. She must disappear for me to become visible. She was the black hole, the vacuum. She had sucked all my light and all my worth into herself. That was when I began to make plans. Once I had my home, she would flicker out.

MOLLY: Things are not looking good for Gwen at this point, but they're not looking good for Fiona either. Mo is obsessed with the woman. We've just heard, that regardless of how this turns out, he's not going to be happy until she disappears.

Let's get back into it. Here's Gwen again.

1.6.3

GWEN ROCKED EMILY, back and forth, back and forth, in the white rocking chair with the floral print cushion. It was the same chair she'd rocked each of her babies in. The day she found out the child she was carrying was a girl, she went to Home Depot and purchased a can of bright white semi-gloss. It had taken several coats of paint to cover the once-brown rocker.

"Hush, sweetheart. Hush," Gwen murmured and kissed the top of Emily's head. Instead of the smooth, blond, strawberry-scented hair she'd expected, wiry strands poked her lips. She rocked harder. "There now, Mommy's got you."

Emily had dreamed a terrible dream. She'd seen blood in a bathtub, a lifeless body, the black silhouette of a stranger in the dark. At least, Gwen thought it was Emily who'd had the nightmare. It was possible that she, herself, was the one who'd dreamed.

It was cold. She should cover Emily with the blanket she always kept on the chair, but it was hard to move her limbs. Even her eyelids felt like blocks of concrete. Straining, she attempted to lift them but couldn't. She tried to bring her fingers to her eyes to rub them awake. Her hands stopped short. They must be tangled in Emily's hair. Exhaustion overwhelmed her, and she dozed again.

She was awakened by violent shivers. The blanket. She knew where it was but couldn't reach for it. Her arms wouldn't cooperate. She opened one eye a slit and looked at her hands to see what the problem was.

They were tied.

Awareness slapped her awake. Her eyes flew open. There was no sweet face haloed by the strands wrapped around her wrists. There was no rocking chair. Gwen was lying, alone, on her side on a concrete floor, hands bound with rope.

The room was dim and shadowed. The only light came from under a door. It was a small space, piled high with boxes. A storage room of some kind.

The memory of the night came to her in disconnected bits, puzzle pieces that refused to make a complete picture: Lance's curling hair and beautiful eyes. The storm outside the windows of the Laguna house. Wine, the smoky taste of Ravish. The dark at the top of the stairs. And something else. Something she didn't want to remember.

She lurched forward, trying to sit up, but couldn't move. Looking down she saw the cords that tied her wrists looped around her waist several times, crisscrossed around her legs and ended with knots at her ankles. She was trussed up like a dead deer.

Fear, cold and raw, raked fingers up and down her body. She opened her mouth to scream, then shut it. She didn't want to attract... *Who?* A face floated in her mind.

Mo.

The wine shop owner.

She remembered the surrealism of finding him in the bedroom. The chase in the dark and then blackness. Why?

Two names appeared behind her eyes: Sondra Olsen and Christina Purcell.

Adrenaline, so thick and strong it burned like whiskey, flowed through her veins. She threw herself back, then side to side as far as the ropes allowed. Her ties chafed and bloodied her skin, but nothing broke loose.

Gwen was no longer cold. Sweat trickled between her shoulder blades. She reached for the bonds with her teeth. No good.

She cried out in frustration, her voice scratching from her throat. Her eyes skittered around the room looking for a solution. A miracle.

The thudding of her heart crashed in her ears. It almost drowned out the other sound. A sound that filled her with dread. The sound of footsteps.

Tears sprang into Gwen's eyes from the bright light. She blinked. Mo stood in the doorway, silhouetted by a hanging bulb in the hall behind him. She must be in the basement of the Laguna house.

Another shudder moved through her. Her gaze combed the room, searching for small crawling things.

"You're awake," he said.

Gwen didn't answer.

"Good. We need to talk."

He walked toward her in short, swift, birdlike steps. This was the first time she had seen him without the ship captain's hat. His hair was red. The same color as her hair. The same color as Fiona's. That detail pressed itself into her synapses, although she didn't know why it was important. Something flashed in his hand, and she forgot all about his hair.

A knife. Gwen whimpered and threw herself on the floor, trying to get as far away from him as possible.

He looked at the blade—not a knife, a box cutter—and showed her his teeth like an aggressive dog. Warm liquid trickled down Gwen's thighs. He laughed.

"What? You think I'm going to use this on you?" He slashed at the air. "Relax. All I want to do is cut some of those ropes."

He leaned over her, turning his head away in disgust. "What a stench. Did you have to do that? I would have let you use the toilet."

Mo flicked his blade through the ropes around Gwen's torso and legs. Then he sawed at the knot at her ankles until it snapped, but he left her wrists tied. She sat up and moaned. Pain shot through her head and down her spine.

He put his face close to hers and held the knife between them. "No fun and games. Not now. Understand?"

Gwen couldn't take her eyes from the blade. He grabbed her arm and lifted her to her feet. She cried out. Sitting up was painful. Standing was agony.

"Look at you. Miss Piss Pants. I can't have you in my house like that. I'll never get the smell out."

He moved to the far wall of the room and pushed aside a stack of boxes with his calf. Holding the razor in his teeth, he grabbed the top box and placed it on the floor, then cut open the box beneath.

Gwen thought about rushing him when he bent into the box to retrieve whatever he was planning to retrieve, but the feeling in her legs was just now returning. She didn't think she could get there fast enough.

As if reading her mind, he said, "If you move, I'll cut off your pinkie. I don't believe they give you a discount at the nail salon for doing nine digits instead of ten."

Mo knelt and riffled around. Gwen caught a glimpse of sky blue fabric, something white with ruffles, then he pulled out a soft beige skirt. "I think this will fit," he said, holding it up and eyeballing Gwen.

He tossed it at her. In reflex, Gwen raised her arms as one unit and caught it. She examined the expensive fabric. Why would he have this? In a flash of insight, she knew. His two other victims had been found naked. It must have been Christina's or Sondra's. Cold scurried up her arms. She flung down the skirt like she was shaking off a cockroach.

"Pick it up," he said, his voice hard. "It's a gift. That's no way to treat a gift."

She'd made him mad. Not smart. Gwen obeyed.

"Now, put it on. Get rid of your underwear, too."

She stared at him stupidly for a moment. How was she going to do that? Her hands were tied. She had no privacy.

"Don't be shy," he said. "I have a mother and two sisters. Had, anyway." He leaned against the wall and began cleaning under his finger-nails with the tip of the blade.

Gwen turned her back to him and wiggled out of her pants and panties, then stepped into the skirt and pulled it up over her hips. She shivered as the fabric touched her skin.

Mo lifted the box the skirt had come from and held it out to her. "Put your things in there. I'll get rid of them."

She did as he said.

He held the box as far from himself as he could and set it by the door. "Let's go."

Gwen wanted to climb the stairs, leave this basement room with its dark, damp corners, but she hesitated. Never go with them. That's what the police always say. You may be killed if you fight, but there were things worse than death. She needed some control.

"Where?" she asked.

He raised his lip in a parody of a smile again. "I said, let's go."

"I'm not leaving this room until you tell me where we're going." Just saying the words made Gwen feel faint.

Mo looked at her evenly for several minutes. Finally, he said, "You think I intend to kill you?"

Gwen's laugh was bitter. "The ropes, the knife. Hitting me over the head. The other dead agents. Seems likely."

His face broke in agony for a split second then remolded itself. "Don't get sarcastic with me. I'm not who you think I am."

Gwen stared at her bare feet. She'd done it again—made him angry. "I'm sorry."

"You think I'm a lunatic who slices up poor little realtors in their listings for fun?" He waved his knife hand in the air. "I am not a monster. No. I am not."

He stopped and wagged the box cutter at Gwen like it was a finger. "My sister owes me. She's taken it all—the attention, the position, the name, the money. Those women died for a good cause, a just cause. Don't waste any sympathy on them." His cheek twitched.

"I don't understand." Gwen's voice was almost a whisper. She needed to know his mind if she had any hope of surviving the night.

He looked at the ceiling. "They were charming to my face, Mister this and Mister that, but they didn't fool me. They were grasping, greedy, self-satisfied witches. I exterminated them in my father's name."

A look of pain crossed his face; he stifled a groan and fisted his hands. Gwen's pulse climbed into her throat. She held her breath for several long moments, hoping his rage would pass.

He breathed through his nose and seemed to get control of himself. "I'm a sommelier, did you know that? Level two. I was born with an amazing sense of smell. Incredible taste buds. My sister, she buys whatever is on sale at the grocery store. She's a plebeian. But she had my father under her spell."

His sister? The significance of the auburn hair struck Gwen. Fiona must be his sister. But Gwen was sure she'd said she was an only child.

He switched the blade to his left hand and flexed and clenched his right hand several times. "The witch." He walked toward Gwen. "We need to go."

"No."

"Don't irritate me." The words were a hiss. He clapped one hand over her mouth and held the knife to her throat with the other. "I thought we were friends. I even protected you from Lance. He was a wolf in sheep's clothing. Did you know that? He came into the wine shop with three other women over the past two months. And he left with them. Left with his arm around them, whispering in their ears."

Mo tightened his grip, and Gwen felt a pinch at her neck. Then he held the blade before her face so she could see the blood on its tip. A sob gurgled in her throat.

"I'll take my hand off your mouth so you can say thank you."

Gwen nodded.

He removed his hand.

"Thank you," she said.

"That's better. Now, let's be allies. You scratch my back. I'll scratch yours." He folded his arms over his chest. "You make sure Fiona sells me this house, and I'll make sure you walk away from all this."

"What are you talking about?"

"This house. I want it."

"That's it?" Gwen's words were quick. "Fine. I'll do it now. I'll write up a contract."

"Not so fast." He waggled the box cutter in the air. "I need time. Time to get the down payment."

Was he planning to keep her here until then? Fear raced up and down her spine. "My husband will be looking for me." Her voice was a broken whisper.

"I'm sure he is, but I left your car at the airport. If the police find it and can't find Lance, well... You know what they'll think."

She opened her mouth to assure him that she would do whatever he asked, but a thud sounded from somewhere in the house.

Mo's eyes widened. He waved his blade at a straight-backed, wooden chair standing near the wall of boxes. "Sit."

She paused. Should she scream? Was someone in the house? Would they hear her?

He took a step closer. The memory of the box cutter on her neck returned with visceral reality. She sat. A minute later, she found herself duct-taped to the chair with a kitchen rag shoved into her mouth. Two minutes later, Mo left, with the box of her dirty things under his arm and shut the door behind himself. Three minutes later, the little bit of light glowing from under the door went out. Gwen was alone in the dark.

MOLLY: He's awful, but I don't need to tell you that. We're back in his point-of-view next.

1.6.4

I HUSTLED from table to table, filling wine glasses and refilling platters of chocolate bonbons. It was demeaning, waiting on a room full of women. Soon, I comforted myself. I would come into my own soon.

I had my first wedding shower at the shop two years ago. Not only had I sold several cases of wine and signed thirteen women to my membership program, but the mother of the bride purchased the wine for the wedding reception from me instead of serving the swill the venue provided.

Since that time, I did showers whenever I could get them, but today was decidedly a bad day. I would have closed up the shop if it weren't for this event. It forced me to open. I guess it was just as well. It would have been a mistake to do anything out of the ordinary, anything suspicious.

I hated to leave Gwen alone in the basement, but perhaps a little cooling-down time would be good for her perspective. The thumping around upstairs had only been one of the painters. He must have forgotten something. I watched the front door until I saw him leave, but by then, I had to do the same.

The bride now sat at a high-top table—princess for a day— opening gifts while another girl created a ribbon bouquet on a paper plate. I used to think it was an absurd ritual. As if catching a wad of trash could assure a marriage proposal.

At a shower I hosted a year ago, however, the most unattractive girl in the room rammed through a lineup of women and tackled the festooned plate like a football player. I didn't believe there was a bouquet with magic powerful enough to make a man want her, but she scheduled a wedding shower with me six months later.

I wondered who the poor slob was. What I wouldn't have given to be a fly on the wall the morning the spell was broken. The morning he saw her for what she was—a gargoyle. By then it would be too late. He'd be trapped.

I opened the last two bottles of the white I'd been serving and realized I'd forgotten to bring more from the back room. I was having a hard time concentrating. All I could think about was the house.

"Oh, how cute." The bride waggled sheer white panties and a matching bra in the air and all the women cooed.

It was obscene. Why did women feel it was not only fine, but necessary, to display their underclothes? If I waved my briefs around like that, I'd be arrested.

I was about to go get the other case of wine when the bell rang. A short, dark woman in khakis and a white blouse entered. She walked across the room with an economy of movement I found both fascinating and disturbing. There was something about her I associated with the male gender, but she wasn't masculine. Still, she was as out of place in this gaggle of giggling females as I was.

"Mr. Cotton?" She wasn't American, at least she hadn't grown up here. Her accent was continental.

"Yes. Can I help you?"

"Investigator Sylla, Orange County Sheriff's Department." She showed me her badge and the hair on the back of my neck rose. I tipped my head to one side and smiled as agreeably as I was able.

"I wonder if I could ask you a few questions?" British, not continental. She sounded British.

"I'm right in the middle of a party," I said, lacing my words with an apology.

"I'll only take a minute. Is there somewhere we could talk?"

I started toward my office but stopped short. Gwen's clothes. They were in my office in the box. I hadn't had time to get rid of them. Even if the detective didn't see them, she'd smell them.

"On second thought," I said, turning. "I'd better stay out here. Keep the party going."

Investigator Sylla narrowed her eyes. "Very well, then. I understand you carry a wine called—" She paused, her mouth pursing as if she'd sipped corked wine. "Red Ravish."

I nodded.

"No other shops in the area carry it."

It was a statement, not a question, so I didn't respond.

"Gwen Bishop purchases it from you?"

"Yes. Frequently. Why is this important?"

"We found a few empty bottles in her listing in Laguna Beach."

Sylla pinned me with her gaze like I was a bug on cardboard. It was all I could do not to squirm.

After a long, quiet moment, she smiled. I didn't know which was worse, the silence or the smile. "I understand the Humboldt agents come in here on Friday nights to unwind."

The change of subject was so abrupt, it startled me. "Ah, yes." I choked out the word.

"What do they talk about?"

I bristled. "I'm not in the habit of eavesdropping on my customers."

"Sometimes we can't help but overhear things," she said in a warm manner, as if we were old friends.

"I can help it," I said.

"What about the tone of the conversations, then? Are they generally friendly? Competitive? You're used to dealing with the public. What are your impressions?"

The more she tried to cozy up to me, the warier I became. "What is this about?" I made my voice indignant.

"Mr. Bishop called this morning. His wife never came home after her open house last night." Her voice became flat. "Anything you can tell us would be most helpful."

I was saved from having to answer immediately by the mother of the bride-to-be. "Mo. More white, please. We're out." For once, I appreciated the high-need women I was waiting on.

I side-stepped toward the hallway as I spoke. "Isn't there something about waiting twenty-four hours before reporting a missing adult?"

Sylla tipped her head to one side. "Two other real estate agents connected with that house have been murdered."

"How terrible." I attempted to look shocked and dismayed. "What happened?"

"That's what we're trying to discover." Her face was solemn.

I matched her expression. "Let me think about it. I'm a bit distracted at the moment."

"Right." She handed me a card. "Call me if something comes to you."

"Of course." I smiled sadly until the door banged shut behind her, then stumbled into my office. The smell hit me as soon as I entered. Thank god I'd remembered the clothes before I'd brought her here. I had hidden the box with the soiled garments in a cupboard with the clothing from the other agents. If they'd been found... I tasted bile.

I'd burn them as soon as I had the chance.

I pulled myself together, found the case of white wine, and returned to the front of the house. The bride was holding a black lace thing with dangling garters up to her chest and posing for the camera. I had to set the wine on the bar before I dropped it. The room whirled around me. I put my head in my hands and massaged my temples.

My mother had had an outfit like that once. It was the first thing I'd taken. One night when I was about thirteen, she shooed me to my bed over the garage early because a friend was coming over.

It had been a hot day, and I'd been out in the sun for hours. I was thirsty. I knew I wasn't allowed into the house when she had visitors, but all I could think about was water. The more I tried to push it from my mind, the more I craved it. Finally, I couldn't stand it anymore.

I crept from the garage and peeked into the living room window to see if the coast was clear. It wasn't. A man sat on the couch. My mother stood by the mantel.

The black thing she wore fit her like a second skin. It accentuated rather than covered her naked curves. I was horrified to see her dressed like that, but I couldn't look away.

That was when I learned some women have a secret art. Not all women, but some. Those who do use cotton and lace and rayon and chiffon to weave spells that can break a man. The ancient Spartans believed warriors should only give into their more base nature to have children, never to satisfy themselves. It's a sentiment I respect.

I stole my mother's bustier the next day and hid it in an old toolbox under a workbench in the garage. Why? I wasn't sure. Maybe I saw it as a talisman or a small piece of armor against the lust that so easily destroys.

She accused my sister of the theft at first and sent her to her room. But after several days of steady denials, my mother shifted the blame to Patty, Angela's only friend, and ended that relationship. My mother ruined most things for my poor little sister. My pathetically weak sibling disappeared when she turned sixteen. Tired of mother's men making passes at her, I assumed. I never saw her again.

Are you okay?" The mother of the bride was at my elbow.

"Just a bit of a headache," I lied.

"Can we make an appointment to taste wines for the reception?

I've had too much this afternoon to make a good decision." She giggled like a schoolgirl and touched my arm. I itched to slap her hand but refrained. I can control myself, which is more than I can say for some.

We made a date, and I began cleaning up after the party, hoping they'd get the hint. I needed to return to the house right away. Things had moved much more quickly than I'd anticipated. I was afraid I'd have to change my plans for Gwen.

As I placed the last cleaned and polished wine glass into the cupboard, the bell on the front door of the shop clanged. I didn't bother to turn to see who it was. It didn't matter. "I'm closed," I said loudly.

"I'm not shopping." The voice was a baritone, rich and rumbling.

This time I pivoted to see who it belonged to. A very tall, ruggedly good-looking man with sandy hair stood at the bar. Something in his demeanor made my blood run faster. "How can I help you?"

"My name is Art Bishop," he said. "My wife frequents your shop." My mouth went dry. I couldn't speak.

He gestured in the direction of the brokerage. "Her name is Gwen. She works at Humboldt."

"Oh, Gwen," I forced a smile. "Yes, I know your wife. She stops in every so often for a bottle of Ravish."

"Right." Art Bishop brightened. "Gwen is... I'm trying to find my wife. I thought maybe you could help me."

My plans had backfired on me. First the cop. Now the husband. If only it hadn't taken me so long to dispose of Lance. "How would I do that?"

"A friend told me she saw Gwen coming out of your shop on Friday afternoon."

I paused and stroked my beard as if struggling to remember. "Maybe she did," I finally said. "She bought some wine last week. It might have been Friday. I could check my records if you'd like?"

"Was there anyone with her?" Art's tone held too little emotion.

Ah, he suspected Gwen of something. Had he known about the lovely Lance? Perhaps I could use this. "Oh, yes. Yes. I remember now. Gwen, Mrs. Bishop, came in first. A man, a few minutes later. They ended up sitting at that table over there." I pointed to a high top nearby. "They had a glass of wine and talked for a while."

"Do you know the man's name?"

I pondered the question for a moment. If I said the man's name was Lance, and later the police found Lance was elsewhere on Friday afternoon, they'd know I was lying. It would be safer to plant suspicion without being specific. "No. He'd never been in the shop before."

"Did you hear what they were talking about?"

"No. I wouldn't dream of listening in on a private discussion. My patrons know their privacy is always respected." Why did I have to keep repeating myself today? I said the words as haughtily as I could without sounding theatrical, turned away, and reached for a case of wine sitting on the floor near the register.

"Listen, I didn't mean to offend you. I'm just at the end of my rope," Art said. "Gwen is missing. I'm afraid something may have happened to her. I'm looking for information, anything..."

"I'm sorry for you. Gwen seems like a lovely woman, but I don't know what I can tell you. She and Lance Fairchild had a glass of wine and left. That was the last time I saw either one of them." I realized my mistake as soon as the words left my lips.

Art Bishop was over the bar in a nanosecond, the collar of my shirt in his fists. "I thought you didn't know the man's name?"

"I, ah, I..." The rage in his eyes struck me momentarily dumb. "He paid with a credit card. I'd forgotten," I blurted when I found my tongue.

He held me there, only the toes of my shoes on the floor, and stared into my eyes. Then he released me and slammed out of the shop, the bell ringing wildly.

MOLLY: Yay, Art and yay, Detective Sylla. I loved hearing how uncomfortable they both make Mo. Unfortunately, they left the wine bar none the wiser. I found myself wanting to yell at the transcript, like you do at a horror movie. "She's in the Cliff Drive house. In the basement."

Speaking of, let's get back to Gwen.

1.6.5

TIME WAS meaningless in the dark. It could have been three in the afternoon or three in the morning for all Gwen knew. She dozed from sheer exhaustion, but pain from the tape pulling at the small hairs on her arms, pain from forced inactivity, pain from the blow she'd received the night before prodded her awake.

Only the nightmares seemed to last for hours. Every time she slipped into unconsciousness, she entered the same continuous loop. She was in her bed in that horrible basement apartment. It was the third place they'd lived after the divorce, each one worse than the last.

Her mother was drinking in earnest now. Empty bottles of gin overflowed their trash can each week. Gwen found her asleep on the couch after school most days. She had to do all the food shopping which, granted, wasn't a huge chore since there wasn't much money to shop with. And the cooking. She was only twelve, however, and hadn't yet figured out how to clean the house. At least, not how to clean well.

The night the nightmares began was seared in her mind like a brand. She'd gone to bed, as usual, in the dark room at the rear of the apartment, her mother still asleep on the couch. Something woke her in the night.

At first, she'd thought it was rain dripping through the ceiling. The second apartment they'd lived in had a leaky roof. She'd felt a feather-light, damp touch on her face, brushed it away, and rolled over.

A moment later, something tickled her ear and her nose simultaneously. She pawed at the spots and tried to go back to sleep. But within minutes, her bed came alive with squirming, scurrying movement.

Wide awake now, Gwen remembered where she was and that no rain could reach her in the basement. She leapt from bed and switched on the lamp. It took her a minute to understand what the small, brown shapes scurrying for cover were.

This was the beginning of her fear and loathing of cockroaches. All bugs, really, but cockroaches especially. She'd gone straight into the shower that night. Put her sheets, blankets, and pajamas into the laundry, and refused to return to her bed.

However, there was no escaping them. The bugs were everywhere. As soon as the lights were out, they swarmed. After a while, the infestation grew so bad they didn't wait for dark but came out in daytime as well. Gwen was afraid to go home.

Nothing changed until a neighbor complained to the landlord. He brought over bug bombs from time to time, which reduced their numbers, but they never went away. For the next two years, until they moved, Gwen's sleep was restless.

Here she was in an even darker, danker basement than her childhood home. Whenever she jerked awake, panic waited for her. It scurried from the coal black corners of the room and crawled up her legs and arms like roaches. It nibbled at her skin. *No one is coming. Nobody knows where you are.*

Her greatest comfort was also her greatest distress. Mo was obsessed with this house. Rather than seeing Gwen as an obstacle, he seemed to think he needed her to acquire it. But the fact that Gwen wasn't the object of his mania was a small comfort. Mo didn't have anything personal against the other women he'd murdered. They'd been strangers to him.

She had many hours to wonder what he'd do when he returned. How did you unravel a mind as tangled as his? He rambled about his sister's unnatural powers one minute, then spoke logically the next. Hot rages erupted from his icy calm. His grip on reality was tenuous. She didn't doubt his ultimate plan was to kill her. At times, she was terrified Mo wouldn't return, that she'd be left here in the dark. But mostly she was terrified he would.

Thump.

Gwen sat as straight as she could and strained her ears. Had she heard something? She listened so long and hard, the silence became a sound. A high-pitched, monotone whine filled her ears. Long minutes passed. The thin tinnitus became hypnotic. Her head nodded.

Thump. Clack. Clack. Clack.

Gwen's chin shot up. She heard muffled voices. A woman's. No, two women. A man's deep rumble. Laughter. There were people in the house.

Gwen tried to scream through the duct tape on her lips. Only a strangled cry emerged, loud to her ears but not loud enough to carry through the ceiling. The footsteps and voices were directly above her now.

Gwen planted her feet on the floor and began rocking the wooden chair back and forth, back and forth. The legs clattered against the stone. She blasted her humming yells. After several minutes, she stilled. Had they heard her? Was help coming?

Silence.

She heard footsteps again—quiet at first, then growing louder. They must be coming from the upper story. The house was still on the market. It could be a real estate agent showing the property. She was sure she'd heard the click of high heels.

The steps now resonated from the front of the house. If it were an agent, she might show the basement. It was packed with the refuse of years past, but still, it was a selling point.

The door. Open the cellar door. She willed them to find her.

She felt, more than heard, a sound so soft it may only have been a displacement of air. Hope bubbled into her heart. One of the women's voices broke into the stillness. It echoed through the basement hallway. It came so close Gwen could almost make out the words.

She threw herself into a frenzy of rocking, stomping, and muffled screams, then stopped as quickly as she'd started and listened for the effect.

Nothing.

About to give it one last effort, she heard the voices again. Not close this time, but faint and muted.

Another *thump*. A door? The front door?

Minute after quiet minute passed. A tear slid along Gwen's cheek and pooled in a pocket of duct tape. The high whine of silence filled her ears again. Panic crept up her legs.

1.6.6

GWEN STIFFENED. She heard the thud of the front door again. This time it was followed by rapid footsteps that grew steadily louder. The door of her cell flew open. She shrank into her chair. Dim yellow light exploded like a solar flare in the blackness.

"Okay." Mo rubbed his hands together like a child. "Next on the agenda." His cheerfulness was as jarring as the light.

The pent-up tension that had built in the dark, burst from its cage. Gwen wept. She felt nothing but relief as he pulled the tape from her arms and chest and the gag from her mouth. She was so happy to see another human being, to be loosed from her bonds, she threw her arms around his neck and sobbed on his shoulder.

"Hey. Hey." He untangled himself, looking uncomfortable. "None of that. You're okay."

Gwen wiped at her eyes with her hands. "Sorry."

"Not a problem," he said, but he stood well away from her, as if he were afraid she might touch him again.

The memory of the past twenty-four hours hit her with unexpected force. For a moment, the joy of release had blotted out the knowledge of who had taken her and left her in the dark. Mo wasn't her savior; he was her captor. She wouldn't forget that again.

He waited until she'd gained control of herself, then said, "Can we get this thing into escrow without Fiona's signature?"

The question was so strange, so unreal in her current situation, Gwen blinked at him.

His mouth tightened. "Can. We. Get. This. House. Into. Escrow. Without. Fiona's. Signature." He said each word slowly and distinctly, as if Gwen were hard of hearing.

Gwen hesitated. She could lie, but what would be the use? It might even provoke him to violence when he found out the truth. "No. She holds the title."

He paced the small room, rubbing his hands together and muttering to himself. She watched him, her rational mind returning as if from a long sleep. How could she make herself more valuable alive than dead? She had to at least pretend she could broker a deal for him.

"You said you have a down payment?" Her voice croaked from disuse.

He spun toward her, a strange light in his eyes. "I've never shown it to anyone."

Several emotions crossed his face in a span of half a minute —suspicion, hatred, longing, and finally resignation. Without saying more, he turned and began moving the piles of boxes to one side of the room.

Behind them, Gwen could see a dusty shelf lining the rear wall. It was piled high with bottles, round bottoms glinting through a coating of grime.

"It's a treasure chest." His eyes opened wide, their whites jaundiced in the yellow lamplight. "Some of these wines have been out of circulation for years. There's a 1940 Domaine de la Romanee-Conti Grand Cru, a Chateau Lafite Rothschild, even an early bottle of Screaming Eagle Cabernet from Napa Valley. It's one of the most amazing collections I've ever seen."

Gwen stared at the dirt and decay. "Why aren't they better cared for?" His awe was infectious.

"This place was my grandfather's vacation home for many years. He was the wine connoisseur. His talent obviously skipped a generation. I don't think my father knew what he had."

"Why didn't you tell him?"

Mo's laugh was low and angry. "I only saw him once. We didn't have a... a relationship to speak of." His right hand balled into a fist. Gwen flinched, preparing herself for a blow.

"Because of her." The hand released and clenched three times in rapid succession. "He only cared about her... My mother wasn't good enough for him. I understand that. I was different, but he never gave me a chance."

Mo began to pace again. "His wife died eight years ago. I called him then. Told him I was sorry for his loss. He hung up on me." He addressed his words to the shelf of wine, seeming to forget Gwen's presence.

She looked around for a way of escape. There were no doors or windows other than the door they'd entered by, and her legs were weak from disuse. She didn't see how she could get to the hallway before he caught her. It seemed hopeless.

"I thought maybe if my mother were out of the picture, he would be more receptive to a reunion. Maybe he'd been avoiding me because he didn't want the complication of having her in his life." He looked at Gwen. "She was difficult."

He moved to the wall of wine and ran a finger across the glass bottles. "So I got rid of her." He pulled his finger away and stared at the dirt now coating it. "It didn't change a thing. Fiona was the problem, not my mother."

He placed his whole hand on the wall of glass and stilled. He stood this way for so long, Gwen wondered if he'd gone into a fugue state.

She cleared her throat. "This is your down payment?"

He turned slowly toward her. "Yes, it's more than enough."

She chose her words carefully, not wanting to anger him again. "How long do you think it would take to sell?"

He closed his eyes, the muscles of his jaw working. "I don't know. Months, probably." The eyes popped open again. "But why should I have to sell it?"

Gwen didn't answer.

"It's mine." His voice held a note of hysteria. He waved a hand in a large arc. "It's all mine. Or it should be."

Mo stared at her as if she should have a solution to his dilemma, but she was at a loss for words. The only way he could acquire this house was to buy it or...

"What if Fiona gifted you the property?" It was the only thing she could think of.

He grunted. "Why would she do that?"

Gwen thought quickly. "You are her brother. And she's not attached to the property. She told me she'd be willing to take less than market for it. Maybe she'd make a deal with you?"

His eyes narrowed. "Do you think that's a possibility?"

Her heart was beating against her rib cage as if trying to escape her chest, but she shrugged and kept her voice casual. "Maybe. She could quitclaim the deed, and you could give her something on the side."

He barked a laugh. "Wouldn't that be ironic?"

"Ironic?"

"Everything I've done to get this house was all for naught if all I'd had to do was ask."

Sondra and Christina's families wouldn't think "ironic" was the appropriate word, but Gwen kept her thoughts to herself. "What about you?" He gazed at her from the corner of his eye.

"Me? What about me?"

"This hasn't been the most pleasant experience for you, I assume."

She gave a minute shake of her head.

"How do I know you'll represent me fairly?"

Was he interviewing her? Gwen had known he was out of touch with reality, but his question was so crazy she gaped.

"What I need is a real estate agent who knows how to go for the jugular, but who is also loyal to me." He grinned. "An attack dog. Are you an attack dog, Gwen?"

"I, ah... " She licked her lips. "I can be."

"But are you *my* attack dog?"

"I want to live." It wasn't an answer to his question, exactly, but it was the truth.

His head bobbed up and down slowly, as if thinking about her words. "How do I know you won't turn on me as soon as we're out in the world?"

"What are your other options?" It was a question Gwen often asked her clients when they were debating over a deal. She wasn't sure it was the wisest question to ask now, but it was what came to mind. If she treated him like a client, perhaps he'd believe he was one.

"Kill you." His head tipped to his shoulder. "But then who would talk to Fiona on my behalf?"

Her pulse climbed from her chest to her throat. "I think I'd be more help to you alive than dead."

"We have another problem, however." He spread his hands wide. "Lance."

Gwen had almost forgotten about Lance, but as soon as Mo said his name, a vision of his fingers bobbing in bloody bathwater filled her mind, and the panic she'd been holding at bay threatened to bubble over.

Mo didn't seem to notice but continued his musings. "I'd thought the police would believe you and he had run away together. Then, after you privately advised me on my deal with Fiona, I'd kill you and no one would be the wiser."

He walked back and forth across the small room, one hand massaging his beard. "But that's out if you're going to negotiate for me."

An ember of hope lit in Gwen's chest.

He spun toward her. "Where would we say you've been?"

"I could say I ran away with Lance but had second thoughts and came home." Her words were rapid fire.

"Then where is he?" Mo said.

"Mexico," Gwen blurted. "He had money troubles and wanted me to go to Mexico with him."

Mo stopped moving and looked at her. "You're very good at deception."

She wasn't sure if that was a compliment or a concern, so she didn't say anything.

"That's not bad, but I need a guarantee that you won't go to the police once you're free."

"I won't."

"Forgive me if your word doesn't do it for me."

They stared at each other for a long, long time, Gwen's hope dwindling a little with each second that passed. Finally, Mo inhaled and exhaled deeply through his nose.

"Okay, here it is. If you go to the police, I will tell your husband that you and Lance had sex before I killed him. Since you'll already have admitted you were going to run away with the man, that's not a great threat. So—" He held up a finger. "For added insurance, I promise to kill your little daughter before I'm incarcerated or have her killed if I miss my chance."

Gwen inhaled sharply.

"I'll have nothing to lose, so be assured it's a promise I would keep."

She felt sick.

"We have a deal?"

She nodded, but said, "I have to use the restroom." She couldn't think clearly in this basement, and her wits were her only prayer at this moment.

Mo's mouth tightened in annoyance.

"You said to tell you." She'd been holding it for hours, and the stress of their conversation had made it unbearable.

"I guess we need to go up to call Fiona. There's no reception down here." His words were filled with reluctance, but he pulled her to her feet and pushed her towards the door.

Ahead yawned a hallway, dotted every five feet with murky puddles of light. Her legs felt weak and rubbery, but she made them move. They passed wooden doors, charcoal-gray with age, on either side as they tunneled out of the airless place. One of them was open, and the smell of mold and rotting wood sighed from the space like sour breath. Nausea rolled in Gwen's stomach.

Her thighs burned as she climbed the stairs at the end of the passage, but she rejoiced in the discomfort. Every riser was a step toward freedom —she hoped.

When she emerged into the open air, she almost wept again. The last rays of the sun lit the foyer and the living room beyond with a rosy glow. She couldn't remember ever seeing anything as beautiful.

Mo walked with her to the guest bathroom. The candle she'd placed on the sink yesterday morning was still there, like a relic of an earlier age.

She hurried in, her bladder full to bursting, and tried to push the door shut behind her. Mo stuck his foot in the doorway.

"Can I have some privacy?" she asked.

"I don't want you trying to get away." He pointed at a window in the far wall.

Gwen lifted her hands. They were still tied. He shrugged and turned his back but left the door open. She was past modesty.

When she was done, she walked to the window. It was much too small to fit through, but she managed to unlock it and lifted it open with tied hands. Sea air brushed past her face, clean and bracing. She swallowed deep gulps.

"What are you doing?" It was Mo's voice.

She spun, expecting to see him in the doorway, but it was empty. Gwen moved forward quietly and stepped into the hallway. From where she stood, she could just see into the living room. Mo was moving quickly toward a woman whose back was to him.

A woman with long red hair. It was Fiona.

MOLLY: Wow. What is Fiona doing there? And does Mo realize it's her? Let's pick it up from his point of view.

1.6.7

THIRST CAME SO SUDDENLY, it surprised me. Too much talking, too much hurrying around, too much stress, I supposed. I glanced through the bathroom door at Gwen squatting on the pot. She wasn't going anywhere, so I hurried into the kitchen and filled a glass at the tap.

As I drank, I watched the sun dip into the ocean. Streaks of red and purple slashed the sky, reminding me of the deeds I'd done to acquire this house. I didn't think they were for naught, regardless of what Gwen said. She'd say anything at this point. She was fighting for her life.

Would her plan work? Or was it a Hail Mary? A last-ditch effort to save her pathetic life? We both know Fiona is a greedy thing. I recognized that the first time I laid eyes on her. A little princess on the hill. Daddy's little girl.

I slammed the glass onto the counter so hard it cracked, and what was left of the water spilled across the tile. *Calm down.* It wouldn't do to get myself into a fury. All the mistakes I'd made the past twenty-four hours came because I'd given into emotion.

In retrospect, I shouldn't have killed Lance, shouldn't have kidnapped Gwen. I'd lost control. The ups and downs of the past few weeks had blurred my vision, taken my eyes off the prize. Gwen had become the enemy I needed to defeat.

But she wasn't my main objective. I inhaled a four count and exhaled on eight, three times. Reframe. Recalibrate.

You could have avoided all this. The voice in my mind sounded like my mother's. I wouldn't be pulled into one of her arguments.

Yes, if I'd worked more quickly to remove the treasure, I might have gotten a down payment and acquired this property the old-fashioned way. But self-flagellation was useless. I grabbed a dish towel from the oven door and began mopping up the water and shards of glass.

I might have ruined the wine if I'd done that. It was fragile. It had to be transported properly and stored in the right climate. I simply didn't have a wine refrigerator large enough.

You could have rented room in a facility, she spoke again.

Why hadn't I?

I held the dish towel over the trash, dropped the broken glass into it, then shook the towel. "I don't want to sell it." I said the words out loud. They sounded whiny and pathetic to my ears. "It's the only thing my father ever gave me, and it's precious."

Did he give it to you? Or did he simply die without telling anyone it was there?

"That would be too coincidental. He knew the life path I'd chosen." Why was I arguing with her?

He didn't care about you. Why would you think he followed your career?

"Shut up. Shut up. Shut up." I was done with this conversation.

You dragged your feet, and now you have to rely on Gwen Bishop, of all people, to work her magic on your behalf. She was mocking me.

An image of Gwen sitting across a conference table from Fiona, mirror images of one another, popped into my mind. Gwen was presenting my case. I was a long-lost, much neglected brother who wanted to take on the property that had become such a nightmare.

I would use all the charm I normally saved for customers to promise financial remuneration in the future because, of course, we would have a future together. We were family, weren't we?

"I think it could work," I said. "I could be the hero. I could sweep in to save poor Fiona from the horrors of the beach house. Slay the dragons for her."

A sharp bite in my palm was my only answer. I glanced down to see blood oozing into the dish towel. I had been wringing it in my hands without realizing and a stray shard must have stabbed me.

I held my hand up to the window. A small sliver of glass protruded from it. As I extracted it, a terrible fear came over me. What had I missed? What tiny shard had I overlooked that might come back to bite me?

A bang broke the silence. I dropped the dish towel and turned toward the doorway. I'd left Gwen alone too long.

I hurried toward the sound, and as I turned the corner, I saw movement in the living room. One of the French doors wavered in the wind coming off the ocean. She stood in the doorway, long red hair glowing in the dying sunlight.

She'd finished in the bathroom and was trying to escape. Did she not understand what I would do to her and her family if she didn't help me? Did she think my threats were empty?

I strode toward her. "What are you doing?"

She stilled at the sound of my voice but didn't turn. She knew she was caught. I opened my mouth to tell her so, but before I could speak, I felt a whoosh of air on my neck, then pain.

MOLLY: Here's Gwen again.

1.6.8

MO STAGGERED. His hands flew to his head. Gwen shifted the For Sale sign to her shoulder like a batter getting ready to swing. The metal was light, which made it easy to use but not very effective. She hit him again. This time, he dropped to his knees. When his hands hit the floor, she saw blood between his fingers.

Fiona spun to face them, her eyes wide and terrified. "Help me," Gwen said, but Fiona didn't move. She appeared to be in shock.

Gwen threw herself onto Mo's back, still clutching the sign with one hand. He thudded flat with an oof of breath. She quickly anchored his arms to the wood with her knees, and he stilled.

Had she struck him hard enough to render him unconscious? If so, it would only be for a moment. The sign wasn't heavy enough to be a lethal weapon. They had to work fast.

"There's rope in the cellar." Gwen's words were directed at Fiona, but she didn't seem to hear them. Her mouth hung open, her face a blank. "Fiona!" Gwen yelled this time.

Fiona startled. Her eyes darted to Gwen's face.

"Rope. Cellar. In the room at the end of the hall."

Fiona gave her a spasmodic nod and ran toward the foyer. Gwen shouldn't have watched her go, shouldn't have stopped paying attention to the man beneath her. Mo turned like a cat, almost as if his body detached from his skin, the muscles and sinew moving inside their casing. All at once, he was on top of her. Then she heard the click of the box cutter.

She dropped the sign and grabbed Mo's knife arm. The man was stronger than he looked, his muscles all strings and wires. She strained at his arm with everything she had, but the box cutter made steady progress toward her face. Where was Fiona? What was taking her so long?

"Fiona. Hurry," she yelled toward the empty hallway.

If she could get a leg up, she could pull Mo down. But her pelvis was pinned.

Gwen focused on working her right hip, inch by inch, out from under the monster. Time crawled. She lost all sense of its passing. She was on the playground again, Tanya Johnson's nails clawing toward her eyes. Gwen's world became the contorted face and the sharp thing above her.

Long minutes later, how many she hadn't a clue, she heard a snap. Her hip popped free. The pain brought her back to the present. In one swift movement, she kicked up, hooked Mo around the chest and rolled with the momentum. It was a move Alan Grossman had taught her when she was ten. She almost laughed when it worked. Mo was down now, Gwen on top.

She reached for his arms. Before she could pin them, a sting shot into her right thigh. She slapped at her leg leaving her face exposed.

Silver flashed.

Torture pierced her shoulder.

Gwen screamed out the pain.

Fuel-injected rage surged through her bloodstream. Her vision tunneled. All she saw was Mo's face. This was the monster that had killed Sondra and Christina and Lance. The thing that held her captive in a dark cellar. The evil that threatened her child.

She threw Mo off with one desperate heave and yanked the razor blade from her shoulder. Immediately, the scent of iron hit her nostrils, and sticky heat covered her hand.

One palm on the floor, one on her injured thigh, she pushed to her feet. The monster followed. They backed apart and began to circle. Gwen held the blade in her right hand.

Mo hunched, readying himself to spring. The fading daylight turned his eyes red like an animal's. But he was no animal. Animals did things because of need or instinct. There was no evil in them. The monster before her was evil.

"I'll kill you." Gwen warned him because she should. Because she wanted to do it, wanted to see the light fade from those red eyes, see them turn pale blue and lifeless.

Mo lunged forward.

She lashed out with the box cutter at the same time something whistled through the air and slammed into the side of the monster's head. He lurched, and Gwen saw Fiona standing behind him, the sign gripped in her hands.

Gwen threw herself at him again, following the direction he'd staggered. He fell to the floor once more. Exhausted and bleeding, Gwen lay on top of him, trying to hold him down with her body weight. It was all she could do. The adrenaline that had strengthened her was flowing out with the blood from her wounds.

Mo began to move, and a sob escaped from Gwen's lips. Hopelessness descended like a curtain. She was in the basement again, but whether it was the apartment she'd once lived in or the cellar of the Laguna house, she couldn't be sure. It was hard to see. Sweat poured from her forehead into her eyes.

All her focus was on the box cutter. It lay on the floor only inches away from Mo's hand. His fingers, which had been still, animated and began to crawl toward the knife. She stared with a cross between fascination and horror.

The hand reminded her of a tarantula she'd once seen in the desert. Fine red hairs sprung from its back. It's finger-legs crept forward with purpose. It was hunting.

She knew she should do something, stomp on it, kill it, stop it from reaching the knife, but her body was no longer listening to her brain. Sondra and Christina's faces appeared in her mind. They were calling her. She was so tired. Too tired to fight any longer.

When the spider-hand touched the knife with one finger, she

accepted her fate. It was over. Her chest filled with an ache much worse than the pain of her injuries. Her eyes began to close.

A shadow moved across her face. Her eyes flew open. Something sliced through the air so close she felt its wind. She heard a terrible squelch, and her gaze slid to the spider. It was impaled.

It was pinned to the floor by the sharp end of her For Sale sign. Gwen would have laughed if she had the energy. She'd forgotten about Fiona. Forgotten she had an ally.

Mo roared in pain, and his voice merged with another sound. It took her a moment to recognize it was the growing howl of a siren. Right before the world went black, she heard footsteps running on the wood floor. Someone yelled, "Police," and she gave in to the dark.

MOLLY: Fade to black. Gwen is a bad-ass, right? She fought Mo until the police arrived. Crazy story.

I don't think I'd have been able to do what she did. How about you? I'd love to hear your comments.

How has Gwen coped with the aftermath of all this? Did she and Art stay together? Where's Mo these days? I'll answer all these questions in the final episode.

Join me next time for more *Murders Under the Sun.*

(cue music)

VO: This episode is sponsored by Greener Pastures Mortuary, your place of eternal rest; performing funerals, burials, and weddings since 1942. *Murders Under the Sun* is edited by Jim Wilbourne, theme music is by Eclectic Blends, and I'm your host, Molly Shure.

part eight

MURDERS UNDER THE SUN
SEASON ONE; EPISODE SEVEN

MOLLY: Welcome back to *Murders Under the Sun*. I'm Molly Shure, your host.

Well, I hope I've redeemed myself. Last week we ended the episode with Gwen's rescue so you could sleep at night.

This week, the plan is to wrap up all the loose threads. We'll talk about the long term effects this kind of experience can have. How victims of violent crimes recover. How their families recover.

And in this specific case, did Gwen suffer with PTSD? Did she and Art remain together, or did the events of the story tear their marriage apart? Keep listening and you'll find out.

The thing I found the most fascinating about this part of the interview were Gwen's musings about her last visit to the cliff house. She asks the same questions I asked in the season intro. Was there a force in that basement? Some bit of psychic energy left from the horror that had occurred there? Or was that her imagination?

If the other crimes I'm planning to explore in future seasons hadn't occurred, I'd say it was the latter. Now, I'm not so sure. Listen and decide for yourself.

I'll pop back at the end of the episode to let you know where we're headed in Season Two.

"YOU'VE LOST A LOT OF BLOOD." Detective Sylla stood next to Gwen's bed. "Are you sure you're up to making a statement?"

"I am." Gwen pushed herself into the pillows of the hospital bed.

"Here," Art said. He hit a button, and the head of the bed began to rise.

Gwen reached for the glass of water on the side table, took a long sip, and began. "The roaches were the first thing that happened."

She told Sylla about the bugs and the rat and her dawning belief that someone was trying to sabotage the sale of the house. When she got to the part of the story where she'd found the opossum laid out the way Sondra's body had been, Art groaned.

"Why didn't you shut things down, Gwen?" His eyes bored into hers.

She gave a small shake of her head. "It was a challenge. I couldn't let him win."

"You didn't know who *him* was at the time?" Sylla obviously wanted to get back on track.

"No. I thought it was Don Gordon, one of the agents at my office. He's—"

She broke off. It sounded so absurd to say the word competitive now, in the face of what had happened. Competitive didn't kidnap and murder people. "Competitive," she finally said because it was the truth and today was all about telling the truth.

She continued the narrative without emotion, until she came to the bit about Lance going upstairs to take a bath. Gwen paused, very aware of Art's eyes on her face. "He wanted me to take a bath with him." The words came out quietly.

Her gaze darted to Art's face. "I wasn't going to do it. I was going to leave when he went upstairs." Art's jaw tightened, but he didn't speak.

Gwen took another pull on her straw, then dropped the cup to her lap. "I couldn't do that, though. He'd been texting me. Expecting me to..."

This sounded terrible. She knew how Art must be feeling. Angry. Betrayed. Hurt. All the things she'd felt in the alley days ago. But she pressed on. He had to know. There could be no healing in their marriage without the truth. "So I went up. I was going to tell him I couldn't do this, that I was leaving, but he was dead." She paused, then added, "In the tub."

A vision of his fingers bobbing in the water filled her mind, and her hand went to her mouth, just as it had when she'd stood by the bathtub.

"I turned to run." She spoke quickly, feeling the adrenaline of that night. "If he wasn't the one texting, that person was still there somewhere. Right?" The fear of the moment returned, and she squeezed her eyes shut.

A hand gripped hers. Her eyes fluttered open and saw her husband's hand on her own. Her gaze shot to his face. Instead of anger, hurt and all the emotions she knew he must feel, she saw love. He gave her an encouraging smile.

Gwen told her story without too many pauses after that, finishing with the arrival of Fiona at the house. "He thought she was me, so I was able to sneak up on him."

"You put up quite a fight, based on his injuries," Sylla said with something like admiration in her tone.

"Fiona did, too. She was the one who—" Gwen made a driving motion with her hands. "Pinned him, like a bug."

Sylla acknowledged the comment with her eyebrows. "Like a bug," she agreed. She stood and patted the blanket over Gwen's leg. "You look knackered. I think we have enough for now."

Anxiety came over Gwen as she watched the detective walk out of the hospital room. She didn't want to be alone with Art. What could she say? She'd come so close to betraying him. Blaming it on what she'd seen in the alley seemed petty.

"Detective," she called after her.

Sylla turned in the doorway.

"How did the police know to come when they did?"

"Your ally, Fiona. She called 911."

"Must have been when she went for the rope."

Sylla gave her a small smile and walked out the door. The beeping of hospital machines seemed louder suddenly. Gwen lifted her cup to her lips and drank. After a long, quiet moment, she turned her head so she could look at her husband. "Art."

He held up a hand. "We don't have to talk about this now. We can wait until you're feeling stronger."

"No, I want to." She gripped the water glass. "There is no excuse, none, but I was jealous. I felt abandoned."

Art's eyes filled with confusion. "Jealous? Of who?"

"Olivia Richards." Gwen stared at the water in her hands. "You were so... all you could talk about was Brian and Olivia. You spent so much time with them."

"I know. I—"

Gwen interrupted him. "Let me finish. One day last week, or maybe it was the week before. Time is all off for me." She paused to get her bearings. "Anyway, I went to your office. I felt like I'd been hard on you. Like I hadn't been understanding enough. I wanted to take you out to lunch, apologize, but you weren't there."

Gwen allowed the words to sit for a moment as she mustered her resolve to continue. What happened next seemed so shameful. Why hadn't she revealed herself as soon as she'd seen Art and Olivia? Why hadn't she spoken up immediately? "Millie said you were at Enzo's."

A wave of concern washed over Art's face, but he didn't speak.

"So I went to Enzo's. I had to park around back, and when I was walking through the alley to the entrance, I saw—"

"Me and Olivia." Art had dropped his head into one hand and massaged his forehead. "I can explain."

"Good. I want you to, but let me say my piece first."

He nodded.

"It was a perfect storm. You were unavailable, possibly cheating."

"I wasn't—"

She held up a hand. "I never really believed it, but at the time—I don't know—I was feeling insecure. My dad—"

"Left your mom for another woman."

"Right."

"I'm not your dad."

"Lots of men have done it."

"I'm not lots of men."

"Fear isn't always rational."

Art acknowledged her comment with a tip of his head.

"There were two storm fronts," she said. "You and Olivia and my anxiety about that, and Lance."

Art's mouth tightened when she said Lance's name.

"Maricela tried to warn me about him, but I wouldn't listen. She said he was a player. I think it was a game to him. Get as many women to sleep with him as he could. Add notches to his tool belt."

"Did you?" Art's words were soft.

"Did I what?"

"Sleep with him?"

"No." Gwen nearly shouted the word. "No." She repeated it for emphasis. "I'm not going to tell you I didn't think about it. I was... mad at you. But when it came down to it, I couldn't."

Art didn't respond. He studied his hands that lay in his lap.

"I kissed him," she said.

His eyes jerked toward hers.

She hurried on. "That's it. That's the worst that happened. I shouldn't have done it. It was a terrible thing to do, but that's when I knew I couldn't cheat on you. It, sort of, made the whole thing real."

"You kissed him." It wasn't a question. Art seemed to be chewing on the information, absorbing it like a particularly unpleasant bite of food.

After a long moment, he inhaled and exhaled slowly. "I guess that's no worse than what I did."

Gwen's heart grew heavy in her chest. She wanted to tell him to stop talking. She didn't want to hear it if he'd betrayed her, but her mouth was too dry to speak.

"I allowed Olivia Richards to believe she and I might be a thing one day. Hell, I even encouraged it." He glanced at Gwen, then returned his gaze to his hands. "Not purposefully, though. In the beginning, I was just assuaging my guilt by visiting Brian and being a support. But she was so alone, so distraught... "

"And I'm neither of those things," Gwen said quietly.

"Right. You were off and running with your new listing. You seemed so confident, so together. You didn't need me. Olivia did."

Gwen huffed a small laugh. "I did need you. I was frightened by all the things that were happening, but I couldn't admit it."

"I wish I'd known." His head wagged side to side, slowly and sadly. "I didn't fully realize what I'd done until that day in the alley. Olivia made a comment. She said something like your wife doesn't know what she's losing."

Gwen sat up straighter. "What she's losing? She said that?"

He nodded. "I couldn't figure out what she meant for a minute, then it hit me. She believed I'd fallen out of love with you and that I'd fallen for her."

"And had you?"

"I hate that expression." Art's face clouded. "I shouldn't have used it. Love is a decision, a commitment, not something you trip over. Was I upset with you? Did I feel the distance between us? Yes, to both. But the notion of leaving you had never even entered my mind."

"Good." Relief washed over Gwen. She'd thought that's what he'd say, but she'd needed to hear it.

"It was pride. The whole thing." He waved a dismissive hand. "I mean, I care about Olivia and Brian, but wanting her to depend on me, wanting to be the hero, that was pride. My ego had been damaged. I'd made a bad decision that put Brian in a position to be hurt. Things at school weren't going well. You didn't need me. I needed a boost."

Silence fell between them, and fatigue crept up Gwen's spine. It filled her head with cotton wool. "Where do we go from here?"

Art took her hand. "Home, soon. But right now, you need to rest."

"Forgive me?" she murmured.

"Yes. Do you forgive me?"

She didn't think she had much to forgive but gave him a sleepy nod. Art leaned over her bed and kissed her forehead. "I love you."

"I love you, too," she said to his retreating back. Her eyes closed, and peace dropped on her like a blanket. They had work to do, but it was going to be okay.

MOLLY: That's sweet. Right? Okay, I'm picking up the story a month later.

1.7.3

ART'S ARM encircled Gwen's shoulders. She nestled closer to get out of the wind and lifted her face to the sun. They sat on a blanket overlooking the ocean at Salt Creek—picnic dinner and glasses of wine on a camp table nearby. She couldn't seem to get enough of the great outdoors these days.

"I've had an offer," Art said.

"From Landmark Prep?"

"Yes. The same money I've been making, but the cost of living is so much less in Idaho. I think we'd be fine."

"Maricela could list our house," Gwen said.

"She could. This is a big decision, though. How do you feel about moving out of state?"

How did she feel? She didn't know. She'd spent most of the past month trying not to feel. The night she and Art came home from the hospital, there must have been ten news vans outside their house. It had been hard to count with the klieg lights in her eyes. Everyone wanted to hear about the Real Estate Killer.

The number dwindled over the next week, but she'd worried the food in the house wouldn't outlast the blitz. Even Emily got tired of boxed macaroni and cheese.

Reporters on the street weren't her only problem. Her cell phone had constantly rung until she'd turned it off. Along with media outlets wanting an interview, she'd had two offers for book deals from true crime writers. The producers of the reality show, *The Day I Almost Died,* wanted to interview her for an episode. She'd hidden in her house for weeks and wished, fervently, for her old life.

"A new start could be good," she said, her voice hesitant. A new start also sounded a lot like running away. Gwen hated the idea of running away.

Although she'd been putting it off, she knew she had to make a pilgrimage to Cliff Drive. Soon. The police tape had been down for weeks. An offer had come in. It was from the Goth-looking couple that had been at the open house. She'd started seeing Maricela's therapist, and even she'd suggested it was time to face her fears. Gwen was running out of excuses.

"We'd have to come back for the trial," Art said.

Gwen shivered. He tightened his arm around her. The idea of sitting in the same room as Mo Cotton, even if he was guarded and hand-cuffed, made her a little ill. "How do you feel about leaving St. Barnabas? They offered you the job. And a raise. They really want to keep you."

When the news came in that Art's wife had not only survived the Real Estate Killer but also delivered him to the police, their family had achieved a kind of celebrity status. Gwen secretly believed the school board liked the publicity. Thought it would be good for enrollment.

"I have mixed feelings," Art said. "I hate to leave behind the people who need us."

Gwen knew he was referring to Olivia and Brian. Brian's prognosis was good, but recovery would be a long road. Although the medical report was optimistic, Olivia had gotten news that Social Services was investigating her for negligence because Brian was home alone the day of the accident.

Olivia's mother had been given temporary custody. He would stay with her until the court decided if Olivia was a fit parent. The poor woman had received one blow after another.

Art was rallying a group to speak on her behalf. He'd asked Gwen to help. From now on, they'd support Olivia as a couple.

"You and the kids are my first priority, though. I want what's best for us," Art said.

What's best for us. Gwen closed her eyes. Sunlight turned her lids crimson. She listened to the sound of the waves crashing on the shore in the distance and remembered.

In her mind's eye, she stood on the cracked patio of the Laguna Beach house before it became a place of nightmares. She heard echoes of the surf from that high vantage point. It was a dream then. A dream of things she wanted so badly she almost lost herself.

As painful as it was, it was good for her to revisit this memory often. She hadn't thought about what was best for her family then. Not really. Only about insulating herself. About never having to depend on anyone else. Strange, it had taken a truly evil man to teach her how to trust a good one.

The jangle of her cell phone jarred her back to the present. She looked at the screen and her heart skipped. "It's Sylla. What could she want?"

"Why don't you answer and find out?" Art gave her a gentle smile.

Gwen stared at the name for another second then pressed ACCEPT.

"I have news," Sylla said. No greeting, no small talk, straight to the point. Gwen was still getting used to the detective's manner. "We found Lance."

Gwen put her on speaker. "Art is here."

"Mo buried him in the front yard, under the fig tree. We noticed the ground had been disturbed, but with all yard work recently done, we'd overlooked it." A dry laugh came through the phone. "Stupid, in retrospect. Anyway, I remembered Mo had raved about fig leaves and sin in one of his interview rants, and it hit me. So we dug, and there he was."

Gwen couldn't respond. Her throat had closed. After a long beat, Sylla said. "Just wanted you to know."

Gwen found her voice. "Thanks." Art took the phone from her hand and disconnected the call.

They sat without speaking for several minutes. Gwen pulled her knees to her chest and rested her chin on them. Lance was dead. She'd known that. She'd seen his body. But that night had taken on an unreal quality. Almost as if it had been a nightmare, nothing more.

The idea that other people were looking at his corpse. Taking it away. Would autopsy it. She covered her face with her hands. The nightmare had merged with the waking world. It was awful.

Art's arm came around her shoulders again. "I'm sorry."

"He was my friend, before that night." She lifted her eyes to her husband's face. "At least, I thought he was. Maybe he was just angling for—" she broke off, "—for sex, but I don't think so. He wanted to sell that house, do a good job. We were a team for a little while."

Art rubbed a circle on her back but didn't interrupt.

"He might not have been the most moral man around, but he didn't deserve that."

"He didn't," Art finally spoke.

Gwen made eye contact with her husband. "I don't think we should leave."

He raised an eyebrow.

"I think we should stay in Orange County." She pivoted on the blanket to face him. "If we leave, it's like Mo won. He wanted—wants—that house, the wine, everything. I want to take it away from him."

"It's not your—"

She interrupted him. "Responsibility, I know. But if I help Fiona get that house into escrow, then I win. He loses." She waved a hand. "Fiona deserves it all, the wine, the equity, all of it. And I deserve to get paid."

"I can't argue with that."

Gwen leaned over and kissed his cheek. "So don't."

1.7.4

TWO WEEKS LATER, Gwen and Fiona stood on Cliff Drive watching the man from South County Wine load the last box into the back of the refrigerated van. He shut the door and handed Fiona a clipboard. She signed. He ripped off a receipt, gave it to her, and drove off.

"All that tragedy for this." Fiona held the paper aloft. "I'd have given him the wine if he'd asked."

"It wasn't about the wine, or the house," Gwen said. "It was about your father."

Fiona glanced at her. "My father?"

Gwen moved toward the gate. "He abandoned Mo. Abandoning a child has repercussions." She averted her eyes from the gaping hole near the fig tree as she crossed the courtyard. She couldn't bear to look at that particular repercussion.

"Lots of people experience rejection. Most don't grow up to become serial killers." Fiona's voice was bitter.

They entered the foyer and a chill rippled over Gwen's skin. She glanced toward the open cellar door. A breeze? Or her imagination? Either way she hurried into the bright living room with its view of the ocean.

"No, but different personalities deal with things differently." It never occurred to Gwen to kill off her stepmother or half-siblings.

Instead, she'd tried to build a financial and emotional fortress around herself. If she didn't care, if she could take care of herself, she couldn't be hurt.

Fiona stared out the open French doors. "Devon and I are thinking about having a baby."

A grin broke Gwen's face. "That's wonderful."

Fiona shook her head. "I don't know."

"What don't you know?"

"What if it's genetic?"

Confusion furrowed Gwen's brow. "If what's genetic?"

"His personality." Fiona threw herself into one of the camp chairs Lance had left behind. There were echoes of him everywhere. "When I saw him, his face, his hair, I knew he was related to me."

Gwen took the other chair. "Did you have any idea you had a half-brother?"

"None." Fiona's voice was emphatic. "No idea at all. The crazy thing is, I'd always wanted a sibling. I'd have welcomed him with open arms, shared everything I'd inherited."

"He hated you, though."

Fiona face crumpled. "Why? I'd never done anything to hurt him."

"He believed you were the reason your father rejected him."

The sound of the waves shushing against the shore below filled the space between them for a long moment. Finally, Fiona spoke. "I loved my father, but I am very angry at him. I had no idea he could be so cold, which brings me back to my earlier point. Could this, this sociopathic behavior be genetic?"

Probably. Gwen had been doing research, trying to understand what had happened to her. Psychopathy was genetic, but most psychopaths weren't murderers. She wasn't going to say any of that to Fiona, however.

"It's the old argument of nature versus nurture. If Mo had been cared about, raised in a loving home, made to feel valuable, I don't believe he'd have done the things he did," she said instead.

"What about Ted Bundy? He had a normal childhood."

"No, he didn't. By all accounts, his grandfather was abusive, and he never bonded with his stepfather." Gwen waved a dismissive hand. "Having children is always a risk. Every family line has its issues."

Doubt furrowed Fiona's forehead.

"Becoming a mother is one of the best decisions I ever made. It gave me a chance to change things," Gwen said.

"Change things?"

"I could protect them in ways I wasn't protected. Love them in ways I wasn't loved." She shrugged. "Change the future, just a little." Someday she'd tell Fiona about her childhood, but not today.

Fiona nodded thoughtfully. "That's a good way to look at it. I can't right my father's wrongs when it comes to Mo, but maybe I can change the next generation."

A wave of sympathy for Olivia Richards washed over Gwen as they spoke. She'd met the woman several times now, and despite everything, she liked her. Olivia loved her son. She'd been trying to change the future for him. An idea struck Gwen. "When do you open your new studio?"

"In about two months, hopefully. Why?" Fiona seemed surprised by the abrupt change of subject.

"I know a woman, a single mother, who could really use a new job."

"A Pilates instructor?"

"No." Disappointment settled on Gwen. "I'm not sure what her background is. Forget I mentioned it."

"I'm going to need someone on the business side," Fiona said. "A studio manager. Give her my number. I'd be happy to talk to her."

"I will," Gwen brightened.

"I'd better get going." Fiona rose. "Speaking of work, I have to meet a glazier in twenty minutes."

Gwen stood as well. "I can close up."

"Would you?" Fiona gazed at the room around her. "I used to love this house, but not anymore. I don't care if I ever see it again."

"Thankfully, the Jenkins' don't feel the same." The couple from LA would become the new owners of the house at close of escrow the next day.

After Fiona left, Gwen made one last tour of the house. In part, to be sure nothing had been left behind, but mostly, to put this chapter of her life behind her.

Oh, she still had things to work through. She woke up two or three nights a week in a sweat, insisted on sleeping with the windows open regardless of the weather, and had developed a pathological hatred of figs. But this walk through the house alone was her victory lap.

She'd won. Mo was in jail, most probably for life, and she was free. In some ways, freer than she'd been before she was held captive.

The breeze hit her as she descended the stairs to the foyer. Gwen's gaze slid to the right and landed on the cellar door. It was still ajar, and she thought she saw it sway ever-so-slightly, but it could've been her imagination.

She paused on the bottom riser, hand on the newel. She should close it, but the idea of crossing the entryway and gazing down into that dark passageway immobilized her.

The only way to get free is to face your fears. Her therapist's voice rang in her head, and a sigh escaped her lips. She'd been upstairs, forced herself to enter the master bedroom and bathroom where she'd found Lance's body. She'd walked through every room of the house. This hardly seemed fair.

Gwen took a small step toward the basement door. Why hadn't the man from South County Wine shut the door? A one-star review on Yelp was in their future.

She took a second step. Why not leave the door open? What did it matter? The house would be locked.

Don't let him win.

That thought had been her mantra for the past month. If she was too afraid to walk to the top of the stairs and shut the door, what did that say about her? It said she was still in some small way his prisoner.

She crossed the distance in five quick strides and stared into the dimly lit hall below. You should go down, look at the room at the end of the passage.

The thought was so crazy she almost glanced over her shoulder to see who'd said it. However, as crazy as it was, it held a ring of truth. She'd dreaded telling Art about Lance, but it had brought healing.

"Face your fears," she said aloud and, gripping the handrail, began to descend.

By the time she reached the bottom, she'd broken out in a cold sweat. She certainly hoped that freedom was all it was cracked up to be, because her stomach had just turned itself inside out. Was that something that could be fixed surgically? She'd heard of tummy tucks and stomach stapling, but never—good lord. She'd lost her mind.

There were seven doors in this hallway. She counted them to distract herself. Three on the right, three on the left, and one directly in front of her. Halfway down the hall, one of the doors stood ajar.

Gwen paused. For an inexplicable reason, she didn't want to walk past that yawning black hole. An hysterical-sounding giggle escaped from between her lips. Inexplicable reason? What sane person wanted to walk past a yawning black hole? Anything could be inside, could jump out at her.

She closed her eyes, breathed deeply, and repeated her mantra: *Don't let him win.* A moment later, she stepped into the open doorway, her heart thumping out a rhythm in her chest.

There was nothing there. The room was completely empty. What had she expected? Fiona had hired a service to clean out the basement. They'd done their job. Feeling lighter, Gwen strode toward the end of the hall.

She pushed open the heavy wooden door. A yellow rectangle of light appeared on the floor, her shadow looming inside of it. This room had been cleared out as well. The only thing that remained was a wall of shelves with notches for wine bottles.

The new owners had been excited about the prospect of having a wine cellar. No one had told them what had happened in this room. Since Gwen didn't die here, it wasn't a disclosure item.

They did know about the master bath and bedroom, however, and were excited about it. Turned out they had some connection to a ghost hunters TV show and were planning to film an episode in the house. That was one show Gwen would never watch.

Well, that was that. The basement was empty except for shadows. No bugs, no vermin, no boogiemen. There was nothing here to be afraid of. Not anymore.

As Gwen turned to retrace her steps, something Sylla had told her clanged in her brain like the bell on the door at The Leaky Barrel. Mo had a complete psychotic break after he was arrested. Police interviews were filled with rantings and ravings that had to be interpreted by county psychologists.

One of the obsessions he returned to again and again was the idea that he had loosed something that had been trapped in this basement. Something evil.

Sylla had barked a derisive laugh as she'd told Gwen about it. Gwen didn't believe his delusions were more than that—delusions—but the memory suddenly made her skin crawl.

She jogged the last few steps and climbed the stairs two at a time, trying to escape the feeling that something cold was breathing down her neck. When she reached the top, she spun, half expecting to see red eyes glittering at her from the darkness.

There was nothing there. The frisson of nerves sparking over her body was a product of her imagination, nothing more. Gwen gripped the doorknob and slammed the door with more strength than necessary. Some doors should be left closed.

MOLLY: Gwen's story is over, but it's left her with more questions than answers.

Mo, on the other hand, believes he has all the answers and that there's more to his story. I thought it would be a fitting end to this first season of the podcast to read the final chapter of his memoir.

The following was written two years after his sentencing.

1.7.5

FRENCH IS the language of wine. I've been studying it since I now have some time on my hands. It makes me regret I never left this bourgeois republic for the eminently more civilized country of France. Oh, well. *Que sera sera*, as Doris Day sang.

My study of the language is how I happen to know the French word for dungeon. It is *oubliette*. It comes from the verb *oublier*, which means "to forget."

In the Middle Ages, when one was thrown into the black underbelly of the castle, the trap door was dropped and the prisoner forgotten—not very humane. He was left to rot in the dark and feed the rats. This seems much worse than a mischief to me.

The state has deemed my extermination of some of Southern California's vermin as a crime. I see my actions as a public service. We disagree but, unfortunately for me, might makes right.

I've been tossed away like so much rubbish into the *oubliette* of San Quentin. They say it will be for life, if you can call this a life.

My sister sees it as divine retribution for my sins—my own personal Inferno. Like Dante, she hopes I will descend deeper and deeper, discovering ever more horrific punishments. But unlike Dante, I won't be an observer. I will feel the pain.

I believe, in her heart of hearts, she thinks my incarceration will assuage her own guilt and embarrassment. She is miserable in the knowledge that someone who shares her DNA has snuffed out a few real estate agents. She must accept I am her family, and she hates it. That's a comfort to me.

I should have been my father's heir. I was never understood or appreciated by him, or anyone else for that matter. I've always lived in a black hole. Fiona sucked up all the light.

It's interesting to me that wine, my passion, is treated in much the same way as I have been—buried in damp basements away from the sun. Out of sight, out of mind.

This is where I find my hope. My *raison d'être*, as the French say. The richness and complexity of a wine comes during its time in the cellar.

So, I sit and write my story. I study French and history and weaponry and herbs and potions and poisons. I learn the ways and wiles of man and woman, and I mature. I prepare myself for the day I'll emerge from the *oubliette*. And I will. And when I do, my sister will drink the wine I've made in the darkness.

MOLLY: That's a haunting end to the story—or is it? Haunting? Yes, definitely. But the end? Maybe, maybe not. I still have questions.

Is Gwen correct? Was nothing there in that basement? Or was Maricela correct when she said that houses absorbed the energy of the deeds committed in them? Or is that something we'll never know this side of eternity?

A story I came across in my research might provide some answers. Gwen Bishop told me about it.

Before the events of Season One of the podcast, Gwen had a client in a little city near Dana Point called Capistrano Beach. The woman, Amy

McKee, inherited a small cottage from her aunt and was thinking about selling it. That's how Gwen got involved. But some very odd things happened there to change her mind about selling.

The story was actually written as if it were fiction by an Orange County author, Greta Boris. When I read it, I felt as if I'd found justification for this podcast series.

It's entitled *The Dark Room*. It proposes the possibility that something evil was unleashed in sunny SoCal through the events that occurred in that cottage.

Truth? Fiction? I'm undecided. You can grab a free copy from the author's website. Read it and let me know what you think.

I've titled the next season of the podcast, *The Garden*. In it we'll dive into Olivia Richard's harrowing story.

When it opens, she fears she's being stalked. Is she? Or is she just being paranoid? As you know from *The Cliff House*, she's certainly had a rough time. What she's been through would leave scars on anyone.

Brian, her son, is healing but still needs constant care. Social Services is keeping an eye on her. Her ex-husband comes back in the picture. To make matters worse, someone is leaving cryptic messages on her car's windshield.

And what does all this have to do with the first season? Let's explore these crimes together.

Join me next season for more *Murders Under the Sun*.

(cue music)

VO: If you enjoyed this episode, please leave us a five-star review on your favorite podcast service—it really helps. *Murders Under the Sun* is edited by Jim Wilbourne, theme music is by Eclectic Blends, and I'm your host, Molly Shure.

Get your free digital copy of *The Dark Room* at
https://bit.ly/GretaBoris-book

If you enjoyed this book, please do one or more of the following:

- Leave a review on your favorite book review site
- Tell a friend about *The Cliff House: An Almost True Crime Story*
- Ask your local library to put Greta Boris's work on the shelf
- Recommend Fawkes Press books to your local bookstore

VISIT US ONLINE
www.FawkesPress.com
www.GretaBoris.com

also by greta boris

www.ingramcontent.com/pod-product-compliance
Lightning Source LLC
Chambersburg PA
CBHW061759190726
48289CB00007B/1997